The strange man kissing her was her ex-husband!

"What are you doing?" Chloe demanded, trying to keep her voice low as she noticed the smiles from the restaurant's other patrons.

"You look lovely," he murmured huskily.

Chloe groaned. A man—probably her date—walked in.

"Dalton, you *can't* stay here."

"Sure I can." He leaned back. "Waiter, could I have a glass of Chianti, please?" he called out.

"Go away," she muttered. "I'm meeting someone."

He picked up a loose curl of her hair and watched it wrap itself around his finger.

Chloe felt a familiar tingle steal down her spine.

"Dalton, please!"

"Do you realize how sexy you are?" he murmured in her ear. "I'm glad I made our dinner reservations here where all business executives won't be ogling you."

Chloe's head whipped back around. "No! It—it can't be." She nearly blanched with astonishment.

Dalton grinned broadly. "Just call me 'hubby.'"

Dear Reader,

"Whether you want him for business...or for pleasure, for one month or for one night, we have the husband you've been looking for. When circumstances dictate the need for the appearance of a man in your life, call 1-800-HUSBAND for an uncomplicated solution. Call now...."

We're so glad you decided to call the matchmaking Harrington Agency, along with the first of the five desperate singles who'll be looking for their perfect stand-in mate in the new "1-800-HUSBAND" miniseries.

You're in for a fun-filled frolic as you join Linda Randall Wisdom's Chloe Sumner, who gets a lot more than she bargained for when she hires her "husband."

Look for four more 1-800-HUSBAND titles, one per month, including books by some of your favorite authors: Mollie Molay, Leandra Logan, Jenna McKnight and Mary Anne Wilson. We know you'll love this extra-special miniseries!

Regards,

Debra Matteucci
Senior Editor & Editorial Coordinator
Harlequin
300 E. 42nd St.
New York, NY 10017

Linda Randall Wisdom

COUNTERFEIT HUSBAND

Harlequin Books

TORONTO • NEW YORK • LONDON
AMSTERDAM • PARIS • SYDNEY • HAMBURG
STOCKHOLM • ATHENS • TOKYO • MILAN
MADRID • WARSAW • BUDAPEST • AUCKLAND

To Marilyn White, who asked for an extra-special hero.
I hope Dalton fits the bill!

And for Mary Schultz and Mary Anne Wilson—
we odd ones have to stick together!

ISBN 0-373-16596-X

COUNTERFEIT HUSBAND

Copyright © 1995 by Words by Wisdom.

Prologue

What was it about Italian men that turned a woman into a quivering mass? Was it the way they spoke in those liquid tones? Maybe it was the way they'd look at a woman as if she was the only one in the world who could fulfill their fantasies. Or was it those warm brown eyes they used to their advantage, silently promising hot nights of passion? Along with that silken accent that slid over a woman's skin with velvety intent.

Chloe Sumner considered herself an excellent businesswoman. She was a person who believed in meeting a challenge head-on. She had faith in her ability to handle the trickiest business deal that came her way. She held her ground with associates who had more experience in the beauty business, and challenged them with a show of charm and smarts. It was known Chloe Sumner, CEO of Chrysalis Cosmetics, based in San Francisco, never backed down from a battle. Never let her heart overtake her head. She was a force to be reckoned with.

Then she met Fernando Rossi, head of Bella Skin, who used his own lethal charm like a weapon in his business dealings. She was positive he never lost a battle. And feared she could lose this confrontation if she didn't remain on her toes at all times.

His toothpaste white smile flashed brightly in deeply tanned features. With his puppy-dog soft brown eyes and good looks, he looked as if he belonged on the movie screen. He was a male morsel ready to tempt any woman. Even Chloe, who considered herself immune against such men.

She might be blessed with shoulder-length black hair that complemented her porcelain skin and deep lavender eyes, which glowed brighter than any Brazilian amethyst. Her petite figure and rare beauty made her the perfect representative for Chrysalis Cosmetics, which vaunted its ability to make anyone look and feel beautiful as long as they used their products.

She kept her smile noncommittal as she faced Mr. Rossi, seated to her left. Instead of beginning their business negotiations across a conference table, she had chosen to hold them in her office, using the comfortable chairs and table set in one corner to keep their meeting on a less formal footing. Now she wished she had that long table shielding her from this charmladen man instead of their sitting where floor-to-ceiling smoky gray tinted windows overlooked the building's courtyard.

Chrysalis's well-known lavender color scheme was predominant in Chloe's office with pale lavender carpet, deep purple plush couches and easy chair and pale mauve walls covered with surrealistic drawings of the company's most popular products. A black onyx coffee table separated Chloe from her business opponent, but she felt it would take more than a piece of furniture to stop the man if he was hell-bent on seducing her. As he had been hinting for the past hour, he would like nothing more than for them to continue their talks *away* from the office.

"Signor Rossi," she began, determined to get business back on track.

"Nando, please," he urged in his deep voice. "I have never believed in formality. It makes things that much more difficult when I am speaking to a beautiful woman."

"Nando." She hoped she could keep her wits about her as she strove to present him with a noncommittal smile. "As you know, Chrysalis has become the number-one cosmetic firm in the United States."

"Chrysalis is the number-one firm that sells its products to the customer in the home instead of distributing it through a department store or through a beauty spa," he corrected.

She was undeterred. "Be that as it may, our sales figures speak for themselves. Our last quarter is our best yet and we're continuing to grow. I think you would have to agree that merging with us would be very beneficial to Bella Skin. You aren't that well-known in the U.S. and what better way to open up a new avenue for your skin-care products than to join us where you will have a guaranteed market."

"We have never thought of offering Bella Skin to the *average* consumer." Faint distaste crossed his face. "We have always believed our product is only for the discriminating female. She is a woman who truly regards us as the only product to keep her skin vital and healthy. And is willing to pay the price for it."

Chloe knew only too well what their clients paid. She had purchased the Bella Skin products when she visited Italy last year. After trying them, she could understand the expensive price. She had urged her grandmother to also try them, and after Amanda learned Bella Skin needed an infusion of cash, Chloe talked to the board of directors about approaching the company regarding a merger. She felt she had the upper hand because the Italian firm was on the verge of outpricing themselves.

"I can understand why you're hesitant about offering such exquisite products to what you consider the average customer," she said smoothly. "There's no reason why your chemists couldn't formulate something special for our customers."

He considered her words. "True," he said finally. "I will discuss it with them."

Chloe reached for the file folder on the table in front of her. "Then—"

"Chloe." He smiled his shark's smile as he spoke. "I realize we have much negotiations to go through before we sign the papers, but an office atmosphere has never been what I consider appropriate. I would like to make a suggestion I hope you will agree to. We have a very lovely resort I would like you to visit. Our clients have all the privacy they require and every amenity necessary to make them beautiful. We also find it useful when we wish to test our new products since our clients are only too happy to try them. There, we can have our discussions in a more—" he gave a telling pause "—amiable atmosphere."

It was on the tip of Chloe's tongue to suggest that time was going by too fast to think about having a business discussion in a spa. Especially when said spa was on Nando's turf. Until she saw the speculative gleam in his eyes. He expected her to refuse.

"I think it would be a wonderful idea to see your resort," she replied, standing. "I haven't been in Italy for more than a year now. It would be nice to return."

"Oh, no, our spa there is more suited for tourists." He made a moue of distaste. "I am talking about the spa we call Bella's hideaway. We have many clients who enjoy relaxing and being pampered while recovering from surgical procedures or just because they wish to get away. It requires more travel for our European clients, but they always appreciate the privacy and pampering we give them."

There was no doubt the surgical procedures he spoke of had to do with making one look younger and prettier.

"I know you will enjoy it," he went on. "It's a lovely island in the Pacific."

"An island?" Chloe repeated.

"Yes. We can take Bella's yacht there. I always consider spring a lovely time for a sail." Nando took her hand and lifted it to his lips. "Shall we say we leave in a week?" he murmured, stroking the back of her hand with his lips. "I look forward to showing you all we have there."

"Actually, Nando, I rarely travel alone," she began without even thinking about what she was saying.

"You do not have to worry. I will be with you." His eyes seemed to strip her clothing from her.

She gamely continued on before she lost her nerve, "So I hope you don't mind if I bring my husband?"

This time he froze. "Husband? I thought you were divorced, Chloe."

"No, actually, we recently reconciled, which is why I don't like to be away from him for long," she went on. "He isn't involved in the business, but I think he would be helpful in offering the male perspective about the spa. You do offer amenities to the men also, don't you?''

Nando Rossi was nothing if not a gentleman as he nodded. "Naturally, your husband is most welcome. We offer many luxuries for the men." His gaze warmed her. "I will have my secretary contact you regarding our departure date."

Chloe walked him to her office door. When she opened it, she felt him take her hand again.

"Too bad you and your husband are together again," he said in a low, husky voice. "I would have enjoyed our nights at sea much more without him." With a charm-filled smile that reached all the way down inside her, he took his leave.

"Wow!" Liza, Chloe's administrative assistant, fanned herself with a file folder as she approached her boss. "I think we need to crank up the air-conditioning around here. That man positively radiates sexual heat."

Chloe collapsed against the doorjamb. "No kidding." She looked at Liza. "He wants to discuss the merger during a sea voyage to Bella's island resort, so we'll need to rearrange my schedule."

Liza immediately opened her notebook.

Chloe began ticking items off on her fingers.

"I'll need to RSVP my regrets for that fund-raising dinner the Paines are having next week. I'll also need to make sure I have the appropriate clothing for the trip. Let's see if I can change my hair appointment to the end of this week. Steven won't be happy with what he'll consider a last-minute change, but explain to him it can't be helped. I'll also need to inform my grandmother I won't be able to attend her garden party.

Please rearrange any appointments I have from next week on and—'' she looked at her assistant with something that bordered on a panic that echoed in her voice ''—last but not least, I'll need a husband.''

Chapter One

"You told him you're married?" Liza shook her head after Chloe related the gist of the meeting. "Big mistake, boss. A really big one. Last I knew you only had an ex-husband. There's a big difference between the two."

"I know, I know," Chloe moaned behind the cover of her hands. She had collapsed in her desk chair. "You have to understand. He has this way about him that turns the thought processes to pure mush. I felt as if he was planning the great seduction on the yacht. I mean this merger is so important, but I'm not about to become a sacrifice for it!"

"Now what is it you always say?" Liza tapped her forefinger against her lips in thought. "It's right there on the tip of my tongue. I know!" She suddenly snapped her fingers as it came to her. "Just say no!"

"That's easy for you to say." Chloe looked up. The frantic expression crossing her face caused her assistant to step back. "Maybe I could tell him my husband couldn't come and I brought someone else who was familiar with the business."

"Oh, no!" Liza held up her hand to ward off her boss. "You know very well all I have to do is just look at a picture of a boat and I get seasick. There is no way you'll get me to even stand on the dock!''

Chloe threw up her hands. "There has to be a way!"

"Ms. Sumner." A young woman dressed in a simple brown skirt and cream-colored blouse stood uncertainly in the office doorway. "Ralph down in the lobby just called and said your grandmother entered the building three minutes ago and stepped into the executive elevator."

Chloe's reply was colorful and not entirely befitting her role as CEO.

"Maybe you could ask Mrs. Sumner to go with you?" Liza suggested, earning a killing glare from her employer. "I'm sure she'd be only too happy to help you out of your predicament."

"Isn't there anyone outside to watch over the telephones?" A silver-haired hurricane breezed through the doorway. She stopped next to the second woman. "Hello, you must be Brenda Ryan, my granddaughter's new secretary." She looked the young woman up and down with a laser-piercing gaze. "My dear, brown is most certainly not your color. I suggest only pastel shades. They would be more flattering for your skin tones and hair along with that delicate air you project. That will lull people into a false sense of security. It's a very helpful trait." She reached inside her small clutch bag and withdrew two business cards and a cream-colored slip of paper. "Tell Henri I referred you to him. He will set that horrible haircut to rights. Personally, I would disembowel the person who dared to butcher such lovely hair. Sabrina will help you with your wardrobe." She smiled as she handed Brenda the papers.

Brenda could only nod dumbly. "Yes, ma'am," she whispered, warily accepting the gift.

"I'm sure you'll look your loveliest the next time I'm here." There was no doubt in her mind the young woman would follow her instructions to the letter. She turned toward Liza. "My dear, you look lovely today. That shade of rose does so much for you."

"Thank you, Mrs. Sumner." Liza smiled back at the matriarch of Chrysalis Cosmetics. "Would you care for some coffee or tea?"

Amanda Sumner waved her off. "No, thank you, dear, I'm only staying long enough to find out how my granddaughter's meeting with Fernando Rossi went."

The two women immediately sensed their dismissal and left the office with Liza quietly closing the door behind her.

"Was Signor Rossi impressed with his tour of the plant yesterday?" Amanda walked over to the grouping of chairs near the corner windows and gracefully seated herself.

One only had to look at the former model's cheekbones and strong facial features to know the two women were closely related. While Chloe's hair was a rich black shade that reflected the light like glittering black diamonds, Amanda's was pure silver. Today, Chloe wore hers in an intricate knot at the back of her head while her grandmother's silver hair was cut shorter in loose curls that framed her face.

Amanda's figure was kept slender by thrice weekly workouts with a personal trainer, strict diet and regular visits from a facialist. She had vowed she would never have plastic surgery and, to this day, kept that promise. Her deep rose silk suit fitted her petite body as only a custom-designed garment would and her leather pumps matched perfectly.

From the conception of Chrysalis, Amanda believed an artful application of Morning Fawn eye shadow and Summer Rose blush kept her looking her best. She refused to deter from her regimen and boasted of never having a sick day in her life. Her birth certificate might have listed her age as midseventies, but she looked a good fifteen years younger thanks to her devotion to her physical well-being.

She had hoped her daughter would follow in her footsteps, but Regina Sumner preferred the scientific side of the business and became a chemist. Chloe was Amanda's next hope and, luckily, the young woman showed a business acumen rivaled by few. Now, Amanda was retired, content to rule from her seat on the board of directors where she still kept her finger on the pulse of the company.

"He enjoyed his tour and was impressed with our summer line and what we would be coming up with for fall," Chloe replied, taking the chair across from Amanda.

She smiled. There was no doubt in her mind the deal would be sealed with Chrysalis obtaining all they wanted.

"Then there will be no problem in his agreeing with the merger?"

"Not exactly," she hedged.

Amanda's eyes turned laser sharp. "Are you saying there is a problem?"

"Not exactly."

"Speak plainly, Chloe. I don't appreciate people equivocating. And I especially don't like you repeating yourself."

"He would like to continue the discussion at Bella's island resort. He feels it would be beneficial for me to see why Bella Skin is considered the foremost skin-care product in the world. It appears the resort is where they try out their new products on their very exclusive clients. He has trouble believing they should sell their products to what he calls the average consumer. I suggested his chemists then come up with products they feel would fill the bill."

Amanda's eyes glinted with purpose. "He's hoping to drive the price up."

Chloe nodded. "He can hope all he wants to, but that doesn't mean he'll get what he wants. The deal we've discussed is more than adequate, but I've left a bit of leeway if we need it. He isn't going to get his price because we both know the company isn't worth that much."

Amanda eyed her granddaughter, pleased with her answer. "Men are so easily led. My dear, you are a beautiful woman. I'm sure once you've charmed Signor Rossi, he will give in without a whimper."

"Signor Rossi has more than his share of charm and isn't adverse to using it to gain an advantage," Chloe remarked.

Amanda held herself proudly. "Yes, but he hasn't dealt with a Sumner yet. And we never back down. You must remember that." Lavender eyes that hadn't faded with time pierced her granddaughter's calm demeanor. "Signor Rossi will realize merging with us is the best thing he could have ever done for his company if he doesn't want to see it die. As for visiting the resort, I think that's a lovely idea. I understand their skin-care practices are legendary. Perhaps you'll pick up a few hints we can pass along to our representatives."

As always, the more common term "salespeople" was not a part of Amanda's vocabulary. She regarded the women who sold the cosmetics as part of her family and never missed the annual sales convention held in different parts of the country. Her active participation was what held the company together.

Last year, New Orleans had been chosen for its Old South elegance, and this year the conference would be held here in San Francisco to celebrate Chrysalis's fiftieth anniversary. Amanda was already involved in mapping out the festivities.

"With the cruise coming up, I won't be able to attend your garden party," Chloe explained.

Amanda waved off her explanation. She glanced at her diamond-studded watch—a gift to herself when her company made its first million.

"The visit to the resort is much more important." She stood and walked to the door with a graceful stride that showed years of ballet training. "While you're gone be sure to talk daily to Liza. She can pass on your reports to me."

"Amanda, I'm not leaving for a week," she chided playfully. "I'm sure we'll see each other before I leave."

Amanda looked over her shoulder and smiled. "I'm sure we will, dear, but if we have our discussion now, we won't have to bring it up again." With a brief wave of the hand, she was gone.

Chloe waited until she heard Amanda's goodbyes before she collapsed in her desk chair. With a muffled groan escaping her lips, she dropped her head to the desk surface, cradling it in her curved arms.

"Is she gone?" Her words were muffled as she didn't bother to look up. Once Amanda said goodbye she never came back in.

"She's on the express elevator to the lobby," Liza replied. "Did you ask her to go on the cruise with you?"

Chloe lifted her head just enough to send a murderous glare in the right direction.

"She feels there will be no problem." She suddenly reached down and practically attacked the bottom drawer. Within moments, Chloe had a small air purifier plugged in and was smoking a cigarette. "I didn't tell her I'd told him I was married."

"Madam Amanda would tear out your lungs if she ever caught you with a cigarette." Liza shook her head as she tsked.

"I don't care. I'm all out of chocolate and I need something to calm my nerves." She exhaled the harsh smoke. "I know the warnings—how it ruins your skin and turns your lungs a lovely black. Right now I have more to worry about. Such as what I'm going to do!"

"I have already listed what engagements you need to get out of and began rescheduling your business appointments. I called Sabrina, explained you would need some clothes for a cruise and she'll pick out some appropriate outfits." She ticked them off on her fingers. "The husband part isn't as easy."

"What about 1-800-HUSBAND?"

The two women turned toward the doorway where Brenda stood uncertainly.

"One what?" Chloe asked.

She repeated, "1-800-HUSBAND," gathering her courage as she walked into the office. Since it was her first week on the job, she was still unsure where to step in on a conversation. "You see, I listen to Dr. Love on the radio every night. She's a psychologist who helps you with your problems. The show also airs a commercial for an agency that hires out husbands for social engagements. They advertise that they're very discreet and the address is in an excellent neighborhood. Maybe they could help you." She suddenly seemed to run out of steam. "It's called the Harrington Agency. They've even been written up in the Sunday features a couple times."

Chloe made a face. "I'm not sure I could confide this kind of problem to a stranger."

Liza inspected her nails. "You could always ask Dalton," she said a little too casually. "I bet he'd do it."

Chloe began coughing as she inhaled too much smoke. "Do not say that name!" she wheezed, tamping her cigarette out in the ashtray.

"I bet he wouldn't mind helping you out." Liza verbally tapped the stake in deeper.

Brenda looked bewildered. "Who's Dalton?"

Chloe took a deep breath. "My ex-husband. A name Liza knows she is not supposed to say out loud if she doesn't want to turn into a toad."

Liza leaned over and confided, "The Sumner women believe they are cursed, that marriage isn't in the cards for them. If they do get married, it doesn't work out. So far, the curse has proved to be true. Madam Amanda's husband left her because she thought more of the company than him. Chloe's parents never married and her father left the day her mother told him she was pregnant. With a family curse like that it wasn't any wonder Chloe and Dalton couldn't agree for more than five minutes. Although,

let me tell you, when they did agree they could gener-
ate more heat than the electric company.''

"Thank you so much for the story of my life,''
Chloe snapped, but not as furious with her employee
as she sounded. The tale was an old one and she and
Liza had been working together since the beginning.
After all this time, Chloe considered her more a friend
than an employee. "I'm glad you didn't leave anything out.''

"Only that Dalton is also drop-dead gorgeous and
has the kind of personality a woman would kill to find
in a man,'' Liza went on, oblivious to her employer's
disgruntled nature. "Trouble was, Madam Amanda
didn't consider a sculptor appropriate for her trea-
sured heir, so she made sure he didn't stick around.''
She shot Chloe a telling look. "You were a fool to let
him go.''

For a moment, Chloe remembered lazy Sunday
mornings when she and Dalton enjoyed breakfast in
bed, and each other.

"That was a long time ago, and obviously he's gone
on to do whatever.'' She waved a hand in dismissal.
"Sculptors aren't known to make any money, so he's
probably starving somewhere while trying to concoct
his ultimate creation.''

"But he would be a known factor,'' Liza stated with
a logic Chloe had to agree with.

Even if she didn't want to.

Chloe turned to Brenda. "When is this Dr. Love
on?''

"About nine every night on KZZZ FM,'' she replied.

"I'll listen to the show, hear the commercial and
make my decision then.'' Chloe began digging through

her drawers again. "Liza, you're going to have to make another chocolate run for me. I am completely out of my bordeaux!"

"Chloe, if your grandmother knew you not only smoked but ate chocolate, she'd probably have you committed."

"It helps relieve the stress."

Liza flashed a sly smile. "Sex does a much better job."

Dalton and sex. It was too much for Chloe in one day. She stood and slapped her hands against the desktop.

"I am out of here," she announced.

Liza's eyes widened. "You never leave before seven."

"Today I am and the two of you can take off, too." She smiled at Brenda. "Go spend that gift certificate my grandmother gave you."

"Do you realize how much that was for?" she whispered. "I can't take a thousand-dollar gift certificate to Victoria's Secret."

"Yes, you can. She believes the way Flo Ziegfeld did. If a woman is wearing sexy underwear, she feels and looks sexy, and Victoria's Secret is most definitely known for their lingerie," she replied. "Amanda does this because she likes to feel as if she's had a hand in your transformation. And believe me, if you haven't transformed by the next time she shows up, she will personally drag you out of here and make sure it's done to her satisfaction."

Brenda looked from one to the other. "She wouldn't really do that, would she?"

"She took Marcus Stewart's secretary shopping," Liza said, mentioning the marketing vice president. "The poor woman was in shock for days."

Brenda winced. "I'll finish up this last report and then leave," she murmured, hurrying out of the office.

"She's getting better," Liza assured Chloe once they were alone. "Her first few days working here she stuttered almost every time she was asked a question. She admitted this was her first job on a corporate level and she's scared she'll do something wrong."

She shook her head. "Amanda with her Queen Mother manner doesn't exactly help, does she?"

"How many secretaries did she go through when she was in charge?" Liza asked curiously.

"I believe someone once counted twenty. She would have gone through more, but Selma came on board and intimidated even her." Chloe shuddered. "I used to think the woman knew everything. I was so grateful she decided to retire when Amanda did. I don't think I would have felt safe in this office with her sitting out there."

She pulled her small purse out of the bottom desk drawer and dropped it in her briefcase. She stood. "Maybe I'll even get brave and sneak into See's."

"I'd like to be there for that." Liza grinned. "See you in the morning, boss."

As Chloe walked out, she stopped by Brenda's desk. The younger woman looked up with an inquiring expression.

"You said that radio program is on at nine," Chloe said softly.

Brenda nodded.

"If you tell anyone about this, I will ask my grandmother to take you to her favorite spa for a week," she murmured. "Believe me, that would make a shopping trip with her look like a day at the circus."

Brenda's eyes widened. "What radio program?" she whispered.

"Good." Chloe walked out, all the while wondering how she could even think of finding a temporary husband through an agency. One thought of Nando Rossi told her the exact reason why she would.

"SO HOW IS ONE of the most gorgeous women in the city?"

Rachel Harrington, owner of the Harrington Agency, also known as 1-800-HUSBAND, looked up.

"Working hard. How about you?" Her brown eyes danced with amusement as she watched the man enter her office. "Dalton, you honestly didn't walk out in public looking like that, did you?"

Dalton James stopped and looked down at faded jeans ripped in the knees from wear instead of a fashion statement and a white T-shirt that was now streaked with clay and what appeared to be paint. His formerly white running shoes looked just as disreputable. His coffee brown shoulder-length hair, which had been pulled back in a neat ponytail that morning, now looked a bit lopsided. His dark, heavy brows should have given him a face to beware of instead of aquiline features that had women drooling. Sienna eyes looked bewildered as he gazed at Rachel. He was an inch under six feet, but appeared taller because of the way he carried himself. He always was a force to be reckoned with.

Rachel was his exact opposite as she sat behind her desk, immaculate in a royal blue silk suit with her only jewelry—a gold pin—fashioned in an intricate design nestled on one lapel. The same design was echoed in her earrings.

His grin would have been considered boyish if it wasn't for his pure adult male manner. He held out his hands. "What?"

She wrinkled her nose with distaste. "You look like a mess!"

He shrugged her words off. "I call it protection. When I go out looking like this, no one would think of mugging me. Besides, I was working on the commission for that new import firm that opened near the Embarcadero. Although it took a while to explain to the owner that I'm not into his idea of modern art, I think he finally came around to my way of thinking." He dropped himself in the chair, legs splayed open. "So how are you? I haven't seen much of you lately. Met any good men?"

She ignored his teasing as she had done since he moved into one of the lofts down the street more than six months before. Their meeting at a local restaurant just after he moved in had begun the cementing of a strong friendship.

"I meet lots of very nice men, thank you very much."

Dalton shook his head. "That's not what I mean and you know it."

Rachel did know what he meant. Since she first met Dalton, he had freely admitted his fascination with her business of pairing women with a husband figure. Except he didn't view it as a business the way she did. He felt it wouldn't hurt for her to use it to find her own man. She had once been interested in Dalton on a more personal basis, and had asked him why he wasn't worrying more about his own love life instead of her lack of one. The pain that briefly crossed his face warned her it wasn't a subject he would ever confide in her. When she saw his expression, she immediately quashed any idea she might have had of their relationship ever going beyond friendship. Watching him, she felt a twinge of regret. Even looking as disreputable as he did right now, he was one devastating man.

She narrowed her eyes in thought.

"You know, if you would dress a little more like an adult, you could make a little money on the side. I could use someone with your charm," she mused.

Dalton held his hands up as if to ward her off. "Oh, no! You won't try that again."

"There's a lovely woman looking for someone," she told him. "You'd be perfect for the job."

"You have more than enough men listed in that computer of yours to choose from," he reminded her.

"The pay is good."

Dalton had to smile at her wheedling tone. He knew he looked like the perpetually starving artist, but he preferred it that way. The commissions he had ahead of him would keep him busy for quite some time.

"While my pieces probably won't ever be in a museum, I still do quite nicely, thank you very much," he told her kindly.

Rachel held up a silencing hand when the intercom buzzed.

"Yes?" she murmured. Her smile warmed. "Yes, I'll talk to him." She punched a button on her phone console. "Matt! How good to hear from you." She turned to her computer and began tapping on the keys.

"You'll be available in June? Wonderful. I've made a note and will let you know when something comes up." She laughed. "Yes, I saw how well your school's team did this past season. All right, I'll be in touch." She hung up the phone. "Matt Travis," she told Dalton. "He's a history teacher and track coach for San Francisco Hill High. He works for me during the summers."

He nodded his understanding. "A jock. Not your type?"

"I don't run this agency to pick and choose dates!"

"Maybe you should." Dalton smiled. "The reason I stopped by was to see if you've finally decided what kind of statue you want for the reception area."

"Something elegant and befitting the agency. Can you handle that?"

His eyes seemed to look inward. "Elegant," he said more to himself than her. "Yeah, I'm real familiar with elegant." He pushed himself out of the chair. "How about dinner tomorrow night? Chinese?"

She always enjoyed their evenings out since there was never any pressure between them for anything more.

"Sounds good. As long as you change your clothes and make sure you're not wearing any plaster or whatever you get on your clothing!" she called after him.

He waved his hand over his head. "I'll see what I can do."

As Dalton went downstairs, he managed a brief smile for the receptionist as he walked out of the elegant brick-and-stone building.

He recalled the local magazine write-up about the agency and how Rachel had started it after a female friend complained she wanted to take along a husband to a family reunion to stop the questions about why she wasn't married. When a large property-tax bill prompted her to rethink her options, she decided an agency for husbands was just what was needed. It flourished from the day she opened.

He stopped in the middle of the courtyard and studied the empty space waiting for the statue he would be sculpting for Rachel.

"Elegant," he said to himself as he walked between the wrought-iron gates that closed at the end of the business day.

A discreet brass plate indicated this was number Ten Harrington Court. What had once been a lovely mansion for the wealthy was now the home for the Harrington Agency, aka 1-800-HUSBAND.

With hands jammed in his jeans pockets, Dalton walked down the sidewalk, oblivious to the old-world elegance surrounding him. With spring in full force, trees were turning green and flowering in brilliant colors. The formerly old-money neighborhood had been transformed into upscale businesses with many of the upper floors converted to lofts for artists, such as the one Dalton owned about a half block down. Which is where he was headed.

As he walked down the street, the word *elegant* kept bouncing around in his head. A word that brought about images of a woman with night black hair curling wildly around her shoulders, deep amethyst eyes sparkling with desire and a passion that matched his own. He remembered Sunday mornings when more often than not they never made it out of bed. Or evenings spent exploring the city. Those idyllic months they had together were branded in his memory, although they had happened more than six years ago.

The marriage's death knell sounded even before Amanda Sumner retired as head of Chrysalis Cosmetics and installed her granddaughter. The sad part was before Dalton could figure out what was going on, Chloe had filed for divorce. Since that day, what he learned about Chloe came from reading blurbs about her in the financial section of the newspaper or reading an article about her in the *Wall Street Journal,* and once, he even saw her on television when a local fund-raising ball was highlighted. He turned it off when he saw her standing with her date, another local business magnate. He cheered when he later read the man married someone else.

"Oh, Chloe," he sighed, walking up the brick driveway that led to his loft. "What was so wrong you felt you had to give up on us? Couldn't we have fixed it? Why didn't you give us a chance instead of listening to your grandmother?"

As much as Dalton hated to admit the truth, and wouldn't dream of doing so to another living soul, he knew it was still there deep inside him. To this day, he was still very much in love with his ex-wife.

Chapter Two

The last thing Chloe wanted to do that evening was work. Her briefcase, which she'd brought home, was filled with papers she needed to read. Still unopened and by the coat closet, she didn't feel the energy or compulsion to retrieve it.

Instead, once she arrived in her apartment, she kicked off her shoes, changed into a silk robe in a deep purple that echoed the color of her eyes and checked the oven to see what her housekeeper had left for dinner.

Deciding she wasn't hungry for the chicken crepes, she poured herself a glass of wine and wandered through the rooms that suddenly seemed empty even with Phil Collins's voice in the background.

"I wouldn't feel this way if Liza hadn't brought up Dalton's name," she muttered to herself, sipping her wine and finally settling on the couch. "Why did she have to do that? I haven't thought about him in years."

Liar.

She fidgeted under her conscience's censure. "There's no reason for me to think about him. He's no longer in my life and I'm much better off that way."

Liar.

Chloe closed her eyes and gulped the rest of her wine, almost choking in the process.

Except with her eyes closed, she didn't see the off-white modular couch with dark mauve, cobalt and emerald throw pillows for color or matching chair to one side. The glass coffee table was actually an aquarium filled with colorful exotic fish a service came in twice a week to take care of for her. The paintings over the fireplace and along another wall were bought as investments instead of just because she liked them.

Instead, her memory recreated a smaller apartment filled with furniture that had seen better days. She had known Dalton was too proud to allow her to use her money to buy the furniture, so she was willing to wait until his sculptures sold for the overwhelming prices she always knew they were worth. They had an over-stuffed couch of indeterminate color, a coffee table with one leg a half inch shorter than the others. A kitchen that was rarely used since she didn't know how to cook. None of it mattered back then. After all, they had each other.

Her eyes popped open.

"No!"

Chloe jumped up from the couch, feeling the need to escape. With the same icy determination she used in her work, she went into the kitchen and took the crepes out of the oven. She sat at the small table in the breakfast nook, making sure she consumed every bite, but all the time aware of the silence in the apartment. After she ate, she placed the dishes in the dishwasher.

Chloe spent the evening reading her mail and picking up a book she hoped to finish. She wasn't sure what prompted her to look at the clock, but when she noticed it was almost ten, she got up and switched off the CD player and turned on the radio, using the scanner until it reached the station she was looking for.

"What are you hoping to gain from your relationship, Mark?" A woman's voice, filled with warmth, practically vibrated out of the speakers built into the walls around her.

"I want her to love me again. I want things to go back to the way they were. I know it can if she wants it to."

"But you can't go back, Mark," the woman said gently. "Sarah told you it's over. She wants to move on. And you need to do the same. Think about what you just said. *If* she wants it to. Even you are realizing the truth deep in your mind."

Chloe felt tension coil tightly inside her as she listened to Dr. Love offer advice to a young man.

"Mark, there's someone special out there for you," Dr. Love advised. "You just have to be openminded enough to look." She paused for a moment. "And now, let's hear about a very special service for our listeners."

"What if you're a happily single, professional businesswoman having important negotiations with a major client, and that client has the old-fashioned notion that any woman they deal with should be married?"

"Or said client is hoping you'll be part of the deal," Chloe said out loud.

"What if you have a social engagement that you don't want to miss, but the invitation reads For Couples Only? Or what if you are tired of people asking why you're single, and you want to stop having to explain that it's your life choice?

"If business, social or personal circumstances dictate the need for the appearance of a husband in your life, we at the Harrington Agency offer an uncomplicated, uncompromising solution for you.

"To find out how to make your life uncomplicated, dial 1-800-HUSBAND and ask for R. Harrington, and do it with complete confidentiality and discretion. That's 1-800-HUSBAND. Call anytime."

"Good evening, I'm Dr. Love." Chloe felt as if the woman was inviting a person's confidence with her warm tones. "Tonight we're talking about whether it's healthy to revive old relationships. Our next caller is Sondra in Marin. Go ahead, Sondra."

"Oh, no!" Chloe jabbed the power button so hard she broke a nail. "That's the last thing I want to hear," she muttered, nursing her broken nail as she went into her bedroom. By now, her book was forgotten, but the phone number rang loud and clear in her mind.

"SIGNOR ROSSI CALLED a few minutes ago," Liza announced when Chloe entered her office the next morning.

Chloe felt the warmth settle deep within her stomach. "Did he leave a message?"

The other woman nodded as she stood and followed her boss into her office. She closed the door behind her as she read from the pink message slip.

"He's very happy you'll be visiting his hideaway and he will understand if your husband cannot accompany you on the trip. But then, this cruise will be taken up with a lot of business talks and he's afraid your husband will become bored." Liza fanned her face with the slip of paper. "Still, your husband is more than welcome. Something tells me he's hoping your spouse will not show up."

Chloe dropped her briefcase onto her desk. "How does he do it?"

"Do what?"

"Make a business deal sound like seduction." Chloe tapped several keys on her computer and waited for that day's schedule of appointments to appear on the screen. "I swear, the man's mind is on sex twenty-four hours a day."

"Considering the way he looks, it's natural he can only think about sex. Women looking at him would only think about sex. I would."

"But that's not how you conduct business!" Chloe sat in her chair, looking at the screen and jotting down notes in her Filofax. "He seems to feel the two can mix and anyone knows it can't."

"Maybe the Italians view business in a different light from the doctrines taught by Harvard." Liza seated herself in the chair across from Chloe. "Tell me the truth. Aren't you the least bit infatuated with Signor Rossi?"

"No." She looked exasperated by her assistant's look of disbelief. "Oh, I'll be the first to admit he's very charming and very sexy and he definitely makes me feel like a woman, but what's missing is that—" she waved her hands in the air as she searched for the right word "—that zing. When you look at him, you should feel as if the air around you is charged with electricity. You look at each other as if you can't keep your hands to yourselves. As if the two of you could explode any second."

Liza's eyes widened. "Wow." She exhaled a deep breath. "Has it suddenly gotten warmer in here?

Considering what you just said, I can't believe the man doesn't do that for you."

She slowly shook her head.

"Did Dalton make you feel that way?" Liza asked slyly.

"I see Stephen will be coming in at ten. Remind him not to forget the new fall line when he's here. I'm interested in seeing what they came up with."

"I've heard next fall's colors will be bronze, copper and olive."

Chloe wrinkled her nose. "Not the right shades for people with my coloring. I'll have to make sure a few cool tones are included."

Liza nodded as she stood. Her hand was on the doorknob, ready to leave, when she paused and looked over her shoulder.

"Chloe, do you ever think about Dalton? Do you ever wonder what he's doing?"

"If you think he was that great, why don't you look him up?" She regretted her snappish remark the moment it was made. "Liza, I'm sorry. I find it's best not to think about that part of my life."

"Then perhaps you should let Signor Rossi practice his wiles on you," she suggested. "After all, you're going to be on a yacht that is probably the last word in luxury with a gorgeous continental man willing to wait on you hand and foot. I'd sure go for a little of that," she added before walking out.

"Not in this lifetime," Chloe muttered, picking up her phone and punching in her private line. She used the eraser part of a pencil to tap out a number and waited. "Yes, I'd like to make an appointment to see Ms. Harrington."

"I HOPE YOU'RE HAPPY I remembered to change clothes," Dalton teased, sauntering into Rachel's office in a loose-hipped gait that attracted more than one woman's eye. He held his arms out from his sides and turned around in a tight circle.

Rachel had to smile at his teasing. "Yes, I see you did."

Dressed in light tan chinos, a white shirt with the sleeves rolled up to reveal deeply tanned forearms and deck shoes covering bare feet, he looked presentable enough to eat.

"I'm afraid I'm running a little late today. I have a last-minute appointment coming in," she explained, adjusting the collar to her lipstick red silk suit. "I hope you don't mind waiting."

"As long as you have some new magazines down in the lobby I'll be fine." Dalton walked over to the window and looked out. The multipaned leaded glass lent an old-world elegance to the room. He wished he could have the same atmosphere in his loft except light was more important to his work than atmosphere. "It appears your new client has arrived," he commented, watching a red Jaguar pull into the driveway and stop.

It wasn't much of a clue, but it turned out to be more than enough for him. Enough that he suddenly found it difficult to breathe as he watched the woman climb out of the car.

He first noted a slender length of silk-stockinged leg, bright fuchsia high-heeled pumps and then the rest of the female came into view. There was no mistaking the glossy black hair tamed into an intricate French braid. Her lightweight fuchsia wool dress was obviously haute couture and very appropriate for these cool spring days. Her cameo profile was highlighted by the late-afternoon sun, so that she looked as if she was standing inside a bright golden bubble. He muttered a curse under his breath as he felt the muscles in his body tighten. Even after all this time, she could do this to him.

"If you don't mind I'm going to wait in the office behind yours," he muttered, feeling as if he should back away but unable to tear himself away until she stepped into the building, now out of sight.

"I do mind, Dalton, and you know it. These meetings with my clients are kept confidential. There's no reason why you can't wait downstairs."

"Oh, yes, there's a very good reason why I can't wait downstairs. I don't think it would be a good idea for your client to see me." He turned around and stalked toward her desk, planting his palms on the polished surface. "Let me make this as simple as I can, Rachel. Your late-afternoon appointment is with my ex-wife."

Rachel's mouth opened in a silent O.

"Ms. Sumner is here," a disembodied voice sounded over the intercom.

"Go into the other room and keep out of sight. Close the door after you." Rachel didn't waste any time. She flipped the intercom switch. "I'll be right out." She waited until Dalton had closed the door before she left.

The moment he knew she was gone, Dalton quietly crept over and opened the door a crack. He sat down, adjusting his seat so he could easily see the visitor's chair in Rachel's office.

"Thank you for being so willing to see me so late in the day."

He stiffened as he listened to the familiar voice.

Chloe walked in just behind Rachel, who held several sheets of paper Dalton knew was the information sheets the client filled out about herself.

Dalton uttered a curse under his breath as he noted the changes in Chloe since the last time he'd seen her. Her hair was styled more severely than before. Her choice of clothing was businesslike. With makeup expertly applied to accent her cameo features, she didn't look at all like the wild gypsy he remembered so well.

Sleek elegance like a greyhound, he thought to himself. How many men saw her with her hair curling wildly around her shoulders and her cheeks flushed with passion.

He shifted uneasily in his chair as other potent pictures began to form in his mind. No woman had ever been able to arouse him with the ease Chloe could. Even when she looked so cool he could only think of throwing her on a bed and seeing what he could do to ruffle those smooth feathers.

"I realize that not everyone is able to come in between the hours of eight and five and I do my best, when possible, to accommodate them," Rachel replied, gesturing for her to take a chair as she seated herself at her desk. "May I ask how you heard about the Harrington Agency?"

"My secretary mentioned hearing your advertisements on the radio." Chloe had a slightly pained look on her face. "I guess there's no easy way to say this. I understand your agency provides a husband for a woman in need of one."

Rachel smiled. "Not the permanent kind, of course, but yes, we do. What we like to do is find the right man to complement the woman. Whether it will be for a company function or family get-together."

Chloe nodded. "I made a few calls before contacting you. Your reputation for discretion is almost legendary considering you've only been in business for four years."

"Thank you. I'll be honest. I can't imagine why the CEO of Chrysalis Cosmetics would be looking for a temporary husband."

"She is if there's a business deal in the offing." Chloe paused for a moment. "I'm banking on your discretion for this. We're negotiating a merger with Bella Skin, a skin-care firm based in Italy. Fernando Rossi, the head of their company, is very handsome, very sexy and..."

"Persistent?"

Chloe smiled, unaware her ex-husband was in the next room, listening with an expression akin to horror.

Persistent? What kind of man was she doing business with? Dalton's mind screamed inside his head. He didn't like what he was hearing, but he knew Rachel would kill him if he dared go in there and face Chloe. She'd had a husband and got rid of him. Why is she here looking for a counterfeit one?

"Very persistent," she agreed, unaware Dalton was hearing every word.

"Is he single?" Rachel asked, waiting for Chloe's nod. "Then what's the problem?"

"I don't believe in mixing sex and business," Chloe said primly.

Dalton silently clapped his hands in celebration.

Good girl, he mouthed.

"But you're afraid he could make you change your mind and you don't want the opportunity to find out," Rachel said sagely.

"No, not at all!" She fiddled with her earring. "I wouldn't give him the chance."

Dalton's expression darkened. When Chloe was uneasy, she always fiddled with her right earring. He made a mental note to see if he could find a picture of Fernando Rossi. He always liked to know the face of the person he wanted to kill.

"He suggested I visit Bella Skin's island resort," Chloe went on. "I told him I would be bringing my husband along, except I'm divorced. And I don't think it would be a good idea to ask anyone I'm dating to go along."

Dalton frowned. *Who is she dating?*

He leaned back in the chair, propping his crossed ankles on the desktop. He had an idea this conversation wasn't one he would enjoy eavesdropping on, but he wouldn't miss it for anything.

"So you're requiring someone more objective, so to speak, to accompany you to this resort," Rachel chimed in.

"Actually, the resort is an island in the Pacific and we'll be cruising there in Signor Rossi's yacht," Chloe explained. "We'll be leaving next week and the trip will conceivably last about ten days."

Dalton almost fell off the chair in shock. He quickly regained his balance before he alerted the women's attention to himself.

"Is there a certain type of husband you're looking for?" Rachel asked as she turned to her computer. She tapped several keys and waited until the file she was looking for appeared on the screen.

Chloe laughed. "Someone who can converse intelligently, look presentable and..." Her brow furrowed in thought. "This is very strange."

"What if I select several gentlemen for you and send over photos and biographies imprinted on a disk. You can then view them on your computer and decide who you feel would make an appropriate husband," she suggested.

"Do I have a chance to interview them first?" Chloe lifted her hands, a confused look marring her face. "This is all so new to me!"

Dalton couldn't see Rachel's face, but he knew her smile would be warm and reassuring.

"Naturally, you'll have a chance to meet with whomever you choose. After all, it does take two to make this work, doesn't it? And if the first one doesn't appeal to you, you'll have others to choose from."

Dalton's heart constricted when he saw the dark light shadowing Chloe's eyes.

"Yes, I guess it does take two," she said softly, mustering up a smile he knew wasn't genuine.

Dalton swung his feet off the desk and leaned forward, watching Chloe with an intensity that would have unnerved her, especially if she knew the identity of the observer.

"You've helped by filling out our questionnaire and I should be able to get back to you in a day or so," Rachel told her.

Chloe stood and then looked as if she wanted to say something more.

"There's something else I want very clear about this cruise." She licked her lips. "Although we're portraying a married couple there won't be any..."

"We're not *that* kind of agency, Ms. Sumner," Rachel immediately assured in a soothing tone. She thought of the temporary husbands who had become permanent. No wonder she sometimes felt as if she ran a service for women looking for the permanent spouse. "Please be assured your husband will treat you accordingly in public and only in public."

Like hell!

Dalton started to bolt out of his chair. He would have stormed into Rachel's office and informed Chloe Sumner that he still wanted to damn her for not even keeping his name, that there was no way in hell she was going on a cruise with some... The description was too horrifying in his mind. As pictures, mostly X-rated, raced through his mind, Chloe left the office. He was positive she dated after their divorce. But that wasn't the same as going on a cruise and pretending the man was your husband!

It wasn't until he heard the door close that he felt his mind return to the present.

"You can come in now. She's driving away."

He barely crossed the doorsill before shouting, "What do you think you're doing?"

Rachel was stunned by his attack.

Dalton didn't bother waiting for a reply. "You can't mean to send her off on a cruise with some gigolo who's going to seduce her the minute they're away from the dock?"

"I can't believe you dared to listen in. You know all my interviews are confidential." Rachel furiously turned on him. "How could you do that?"

"Because I wanted to know why she came here!" he shouted.

"You heard why. She came to me so the gentleman wouldn't try to seduce her," she shot back. "And it wasn't any of your business."

"It is where my wife is concerned!" He thrust his fingers through his hair, dislodging the neatly combed ponytail. "She's got some Italian sniffing after her and—"

Rachel threw up her hands. "Oh, for heaven's sake, Dalton, she's your *ex*-wife. How long have you been divorced?"

His dark brown eyes, the shade of rich dark chocolate, displayed a deep sorrow. "Six years, three months, six days."

That was not the answer she had expected. "Oh, Dalton." She reached out with the intention of comforting him, then hastily drew back her hand.

"The divorce wasn't my idea!" he said savagely, whipping around. "If she hadn't listened to that autocratic grandmother of hers, we'd still be married. But between being told that marrying a sculptor wasn't good for the family name and that the Sumner women couldn't hold a man for a lifetime, she didn't have a chance. And neither did I," he added under his breath.

When he turned around, purpose shone out of his eyes like a beacon. It was as if his gaze spoke loud and clear to her. Rachel shook her head in denial and backed away.

"No."

He advanced on her. "You don't know what I'm going to say."

"Yes, I do, and I still say no."

"Why not?"

"Because it's not ethical!"

"She's looking for a husband," he reminded her.

"But you're not on my books."

He looked around. "Then sign me up! You've been wanting me for months now. Here's your chance."

Rachel kept shaking her head. "It's not right, Dalton. My agency is successful because of its discretion. I can't allow you to destroy that just because you want to get back with your ex-wife. If you want to talk to her, call her on the phone."

He took a deep breath. "She won't talk to me."

"And you think this will work."

"Yes."

Rachel turned away. As she stared at her office, elegant yet warm with its antique furniture, bits and pieces of her conversation with Chloe came back to her. For all her success and wealth, she could see Chloe was an unhappy woman. And the comment about two to make things work had pricked something inside her.

"I am a fool."

Dalton spun around.

Rachel walked back over to her desk and pulled a sheaf of papers out of one of the drawers.

"You will owe me big for this," she told him. "And I don't just mean your picking up the dinner check tonight, either."

"Even if it meant my soul I would pay the price," Dalton said quietly.

Chapter Three

"I think I have just the right person for you."

Chloe clutched the phone receiver in one hand and grabbed her pen. She couldn't believe Rachel had come through for her barely eighteen hours later.

"So soon?" She coughed. "I mean, I thought you were going to send over a computer disk with several choices for me."

"I was, but this gentleman came in this morning and he seems very appropriate for what you're looking for," Rachel went on. "He's well educated, good background, speaks Italian, which I thought would be a plus for you, and he has no problem with taking the cruise."

The lump in the pit of Chloe's throat dropped like a stone into her stomach.

"I'd like a chance to talk to him first. To make sure he understands everything that's involved with this assignment."

"Of course, and he wants to meet with you also," she went on. "In fact, he asked if you would be available for dinner tonight. He thought a relaxed atmosphere might make it easier on both of you."

Chloe frowned. She could sense something a little odd in Rachel's manner as she spoke.

"That would be fine," she said finally. "Our meeting in a social atmosphere would be better. Anything he chooses would be fine with me."

Rachel named an Italian restaurant not far from the business district. "Seven o'clock?"

"Fine. Uh, how will I know him?"

"That's all taken care of. I'm sorry, my other line is ringing. Good luck!"

"Wait! What's his name!" Chloe uttered a curse as she realized all she heard was a dial tone. She quickly dialed the number, but was told Ms. Harrington was called out of the office. When she explained the reason for her call, the receptionist regretfully said she couldn't give out that information, but she would have Ms. Harrington call as soon as she returned.

"Oh, well, there can't be that many men there looking for what basically sounds like a blind date," she muttered.

"You have to tell me," Liza sang out, walking into the office and setting several memos to be initialed in front of Chloe. Still smiling, she dropped into the visitor's chair. "Did the Harrington Agency find some gorgeous hunks to set you up with? Did she say the computer disk was on the way? I want to help choose your husband."

Chloe shook her head at her assistant's teasing. "You're having fun with this, aren't you?"

"My life is so boring, I need to enjoy someone else's. Right now, I have to settle for yours, puny as it may be." She flicked a piece of lint off her cream Victorian-style blouse. "When do we get to see the men?

Do you think she'd mind if I chose one of the left-
overs?''

"We don't. Someone came in who she feels is right
for me, so I'm meeting him for dinner tonight." Chloe
barely glanced over the memos before signing them.

Liza leaned forward, her face alight with interest.
"Do you want a chaperon?"

"No."

"I'll remain quiet and unobtrusive."

"No, you won't, and we both know it."

"Are you sure you don't want me to go along?"

Chloe looked up. "Yes." She stared at her assistant. "Who's the boss here?"

Liza merely smiled. "I've always believed in the
theory of power behind the throne."

"Maybe I should ask if Selma would come out of
retirement and help out here."

"That threat holds no heat and we both know it.
Besides, she'd scare poor Brenda off in seconds. And
I've almost got her perfectly trained now. Do you
honestly want me to start over with someone else?"

Chloe looked at the ceiling. "How did a wonderful
employee turn into such a horrible tyrant?"

Liza leaned across the desk to confide, "I learned
from Amanda."

"Why did I ask." Chloe sighed. "All right, tomorrow I'm meeting with the chemists at the lab, then
having lunch with my mother," she said, trying to
change the subject.

"What are you going to wear for your dinner tonight?"

Chloe glanced down at her royal blue skirt, which
had a matching jacket hanging in the small closet. Her

white blouse had narrow blue stripes that matched the jacket and skirt.

"There is nothing wrong with what I'm wearing."

"Only if you're attending a business dinner."

"It *is* a business dinner," she argued.

"You're going to have to think of this man as your husband for a week," Liza unnecessarily reminded her. "That means you better start thinking that way now."

Chloe grimaced. "Why did I open my big mouth and tell Nando I was married?"

"Because you were afraid of a seduction at sea?"

"I'm not even attracted to the man!"

"No, but you haven't been around a real man in a long time and he obviously looked pretty good."

"I have so been around real men! I date!" Chloe argued.

Liza gave her a speaking look. "None of the men you've gone out with could even be remotely considered a date. They were more like business arrangements."

She hated it when Liza was right, but she wasn't about to tell her so. "So is this."

"It's not the same and you know it. Besides, maybe when the two of you meet it will be love at first sight."

Chloe shook her head. "You've been reading too many romance books."

"At least change into something guaranteed to knock him dead." She brightened. "There's that boutique we passed by last week when we returned from lunch. Remember the red dress in the window? That would be perfect."

Chloe remembered all too well. Short, skimpy and something a part of her died to try on and another part of her told her to behave.

"Not for this kind of dinner."

"Why not? All right, then go over and see what else they have," she suggested. "Your afternoon is clear and you really should wear something less business-like. Go do some shopping. You'll feel better."

"And if Amanda makes one of her surprise visits?"

"I'll tell her you're preparing for your cruise with Signor Rossi."

Chloe picked up her purse. "I can't believe I'm doing this."

"Go." Liza pushed her out of the office, hoping her boss wouldn't change her mind or lose her courage. She didn't breathe a sigh of relief until she checked downstairs and learned Chloe had left in a cab.

"I never thought working here would be so interesting," Brenda commented, watching it all with wide eyes.

"Stick around," Liza advised. "I have an idea there's going to be even more excitement before this is over."

THE MOMENT CHLOE STEPPED into the restaurant, she felt as if all eyes were on her. She immediately wished she hadn't allowed the salesclerk to talk her into the red dress, but once she put it on, she felt wonderful. So for the first time in a long while, she listened to her wilder half and held out her credit card. Not stopping there, she found shoes and evening bag to match and even took a chance at her hairdresser's. After her stylist saw her dress, he insisted she leave the hairdo up to him. It wasn't until he allowed her to look in the mirror after he finished that she realized she'd made a mistake.

Outside, she tentatively patted the wild riot of raven curls held back with a red silk-covered clip that matched her dress. Her red silk dress flowed over her body, ending well above the knees and draped seductively in the front, showing a fair amount of pale skin with only narrow straps holding it up. She couldn't help notice the maître d's broad smile of welcome as she stepped inside the restaurant.

"I'm Chloe Sumner," she explained, gathering the soft cashmere shawl around her shoulders in an effort to keep her front covered. "I'm meeting someone here."

"Yes, Signora Sumner," he said smoothly. "The gentleman called and explained he was on his way. Would you care to wait in the bar or be seated now?"

Chloe was uneasily aware of the interested looks from the men in the bar directed her way. "I'd definitely prefer to be seated."

She didn't breathe a sigh of relief until she was seated at a table in a cozy corner of the large dining room. She ordered a glass of wine and, now left alone, looked around the restaurant.

She hadn't been in here before and was interested in seeing the old-world atmosphere with vintage photographs of Italy taken at the turn of the century and menus lavishly handwritten in Italian decorating the walls. As she leaned forward, she forgot about the shawl that slipped down her arms.

"Darling! On time as always." A man swooped down and his mouth covered hers in a heated kiss before she had time to react to the voice much less the words. "I know. I'm late, as always," he murmured as he returned to her mouth, his tongue thrusting inside to create the kind of intimacy only longtime lovers engage in.

Chloe's eyes widened to saucer proportions as she realized the man kissing her with alarming familiarity was her ex-husband. By then, her lips had started to soften under his heated, probing touch, and she had even begun to respond! She started to lift her arms and throw herself wholeheartedly into the kiss when she suddenly realized that might not be a good idea. It took her a moment to gather herself and rear back. Even then, she felt the compulsion to return to his kiss.

"What are you doing?" she demanded in a low voice quivering with fury. She tried to keep her expression impassive as she noticed the smiles from the other patrons as they viewed the loving couple.

Dalton straightened. He looked around with his own smile broad and warm as if he knew the others would understand why he had to kiss such a beautiful woman so passionately. He dropped onto the chair next to hers. His gaze danced over her face and down across the bare expanse of skin. It lingered on the shadowy hint of cleavage. With each breath he took, he inhaled the warm floral scent of her perfume. It wasn't the same fragrance he remembered her wearing when they were married, but no less lethal.

"You look lovely."

Chloe looked around, then almost groaned in anger when she noticed a man just walking in.

"You can't stay here."

"Sure I can." He leaned back. "Giuseppe, could I have a glass of Chianti, please?" he called out to one of the waiters.

"Go away," she muttered. "Just go away. I'm here on business."

He picked up a loose curl and watched it wrap itself around his finger.

"Really? I didn't realize Chrysalis executives dressed so seductively for a business dinner. I'm glad to see you're wearing your hair the way it's meant to be worn," he murmured.

Chloe felt the heat steal down her back.

"Dalton, please." She hated herself for begging, but if that's what it took she'd do it. "Go away."

He glanced at her hands, noticing the fingers flexing as if they were preparing to wrap themselves around his neck. If she only knew he wouldn't mind having those fingers on him again!

"Do you realize just how sexy you look in that red dress?" he murmured in her ear. "I'm glad I made our dinner reservations here where all the up-and-coming executives wouldn't be dropping in and desiring you."

Chloe's head whipped around so fast she was lucky she didn't suffer from whiplash.

"You were sent here by the Harrington Agency?" she whispered.

Dalton nodded.

Chloe then got her first good look at him. His black pleated slacks and matching silk shirt made him look dangerous and seductive. His hair was longer than she last remembered. Long enough to be brushed back into a neat ponytail. With his tanned skin and slight muscular build he didn't look at all like an artist. She wouldn't admit she read the art magazines always looking for his name. Was he doing this as a way to make extra money?

"Why didn't you tell Ms. Harrington you knew me when she gave you my name?" she demanded in a low voice.

He shrugged, only glancing away long enough to smile his thanks at the waiter who set the wineglass in front of him.

"You needed a husband for a business cruise. Can you think of a better choice than a man who's been married to you?" He picked up the menu in front of Chloe. "Have you decided what you want to eat? They serve great pasta dishes here. And the garlic bread is made just the way you like it."

Chloe felt herself weaken. Dalton knew exactly what buttons to push.

"I try to keep my carbohydrate levels at a minimum."

Dalton's mouth stretched in a slow smile. "That kind of prissy statement doesn't go with the dress, duchess," he murmured in the husky voice that always had Chloe remembering nights in Dalton's large brass bed with its huge soft mattress. Nights that went on until dawn. Dalton whispering words of passion, then showing her just what he meant. He ran his finger across her shoulder.

Chloe felt the waves of heat travel where his finger did.

"So Chrysalis is now getting into skin care," he said in a barely audible voice. "When you decide to branch out you don't do it by half measures, do you?"

She looked around, fearing they might be overheard. She was relieved to see the tables around them were arranged so there was no way they could be eavesdropped on.

"That is not for public knowledge."

"I'm not the public," he reminded her. "Don't worry, your secret is safe with me. Rachel only explains enough so we know what's going on. She said your prospective merger is getting a little heavy-handed and you want to keep this all business. Which is where I come in."

"Are you ready to order now?"

Chloe glanced up at the waiter, then down at the menu she hadn't looked at. She shook her head, helpless with making a decision at that moment. She barely listened as Dalton ordered for them both, but she wasn't worried. He knew her tastes only too well.

"I have to admit I was surprised to see you here," she said once they were left alone again. "Why would you want to work for what's basically considered an escort service?"

"For one, Rachel doesn't consider it anything close to an escort service," he told her. "And I do it because it's interesting and a nice change of pace from working in clay. It's not a full-time job for me." He leaned back in his chair and draped his arm across the back. "Where is this cruise taking us?"

"The company we're dealing with has an exclusive island spa and resort in the Pacific," she said in a low voice. "Signor Rossi feels I should see where they first present their new skin-care products to their clients. It's very posh, very expensive."

"How does that fit in with the Chrysalis clients who buy from representatives that come to their home or office with cute little lavender bags filled with all those fancy tricks of the makeup trade?"

"They want to branch into another market and we need to expand our line," she replied softly. "So far, we've been successful without the skin-care products, but if we want to continue growing we need the addition. Bella Skin is the market we'd like. In turn, they'll market our products overseas."

Dalton's mouth twisted in a parody of a smile. "I'm sure that makes Dame Amanda very happy."

"She's only happy when a deal is signed, sealed and delivered." She picked up her wine and sipped, savoring the tart liquid flowing down her throat. "I intend to present this to her gift wrapped."

"Which you can do as long as you have a husband to keep the amorous Rossi away."

She nodded. "Yes, but it won't be you. I'll call Ms. Harrington in the morning and tell her to find someone else for me."

"What excuse will you give her that I won't work out?"

"That we're divorced!"

Dalton leaned back in his chair, still keeping his arm draped across the back of it. His fingers stroked her bare arm in an absent caress.

"You're talking about a cruise, Chloe, my love. Do you honestly want to be alone in a stateroom with a man you don't even know? How are you going to act as if you're intimate? At least with me you won't have to worry about my making a mistake where you're concerned." His voice lowered to a husky purr. "I still remember everything about you, duchess. Believe me, your Signor Rossi won't have any doubts that you and I are husband and wife."

Her senses tingled under his verbal caress. She wasn't going to tell him that that was what she was afraid of.

Her reply was stalled by the waiter's appearance with their antipasto. The man smiled as he set the plates in front of them.

He spoke to Dalton in rapid, flowing Italian. Chloe was surprised when Dalton replied in the same language.

"What did he say?" she asked when they had been left alone.

His lips curved upward. He turned his head so he could look into her eyes as he spoke. "He told me my lady needs to eat more. He said I wouldn't want to lose her to a spring breeze that could carry her off before I could make love to her."

Chloe's lips opened in a soft O. She quickly applied herself to her food.

"Since that's already happened, I don't think you need to worry about it," she said tartly.

Dalton couldn't resist leaning over and whispering in her ear, "Yes, but that doesn't mean we can't find out if that old magic is still there."

Chloe knew a challenge when it was issued. She gazed back at him, refusing to look away when his eyes darkened with familiar lights. She coughed softly to cover her confusion.

"So what have you been doing? Still sculpting?" she asked in her brightest voice as another ruse to cover the conflicting feelings rising in her body.

"Yes." He didn't elaborate, but he made sure his answer could cover a lot of bases where they were concerned.

Her nostrils flared slightly as she inhaled the warm musky scent of his skin. "If you're registered with the Harrington Agency you must live in the San Francisco area."

"I do," he said noncommittally, allowing his gaze to wander leisurely down her body.

"Have you worked for the agency long?" she probed delicately. Chloe felt as if every muscle in her body had tightened to the breaking point.

"Long enough."

"Is it interesting work?" She pushed her food around the plate with her fork. The last thing she wanted to do at that moment was eat. Had he always been able to affect her so strongly?

"You meet some very nice people."

Chloe was grateful when the waiter came to take away their plates and replace them with the main course.

"What do you do there?" She was pleased with herself for asking her question so innocuously. *Were you always this sexy? Did I always feel this need to make love to you? Is it warm in here?*

Dalton had just cut into his chicken marsala. He paused. Then he flashed her a grin that was so wicked it should be labeled illegal.

"Anything that's necessary."

After his provocative reply, Chloe knew better than to pursue that line of subject unless she was prepared to pay the consequences.

"This looks wonderful!" she said with enthusiasm as she dug into her own dish of chicken. It could have been cardboard for all she could taste.

"So how is the world of making one beautiful going?" Dalton asked, snaring her attention once more.

"Very well," she replied, wishing they weren't discussing the business when she would really like to know more about him. "We were featured in several top-name magazines. We're continually signing on new representatives, and last quarter was our all-time best."

His gaze swept over her with an alarming intensity. "You look prosperous. I heard Dame Amanda retired. How does she handle not being in charge of everyone's lives?"

Chloe chose to ignore his pointed remark. "I don't think she's thought of it as that. Amanda claimed she wanted to live an idle life, but so far she hasn't been all that idle."

"No, I guess not. That lady always liked to have her fingers in every pie around her." Dalton quickly changed tactics. "What about you? You don't spend twenty-four hours at corporate headquarters, do you?"

"I belong to a health club, sit on a few charity boards. I keep busy."

Chloe had no idea of time as she and Dalton ate and talked. Nor had she ever remembered an evening she enjoyed more.

"Oh, no, I'll take care of that!" she protested when Dalton placed a credit card on the tray.

He shook his head. "I invited you. I pay."

When they later walked outside, Chloe shifted her shawl closer around her shoulders. She handed the parking valet her ticket stub and turned to Dalton.

"This could be a mistake."

He smiled. "Would it?"

She never believed in quick decisions. Maybe that was why she surprised herself.

"If you give me your number, I'll have my assistant call you with the information about the cruise. I hope you won't be offended if I offer to purchase a wardrobe for you." She lifted her chin, fully prepared to do battle.

Dalton had to smile. He always admired her spunk. He pulled a pen and small business card out of his pocket and wrote on it. "Don't worry, duchess, I won't embarrass you. I have the right clothes for the trip."

Chloe turned when the parking valet parked the Jaguar in front of her. "Can I give you a lift anywhere?"

"No, thanks, I don't live far from here," he lied.

"Well, good night, then. Thank you for dinner." She started to walk toward her car, then stopped. She turned around. "Tell me something. How did you manage to get Rachel Harrington to send you out for this?"

"Funny thing about that. She said we were a perfect match." Unable to stop himself, he stepped forward, cupping her chin in his hand. His thumb pressed briefly against her lower lip, smoothing a path along the moist skin. He dipped his head and pressed a light kiss on her lips and drew back before he wanted more. "Good night, Chloe. I'll see you soon."

She stood there dumbfounded as she watched Dalton walk away. Her lips still burned from his kiss.

"I think I'm in big trouble."

Chapter Four

"Chloe, I feel you are lovelier every time I see you. I can see the ocean air loves you," Nando greeted Chloe, lifting her hand and caressing the back with his lips. His brown eyes caressed her with sensual intent. He lifted his head and looked around. He turned back to her with a hopeful smile. "But I do not see your husband. Could he not make it, after all? What a shame. I had hoped to meet him," he said with open insincerity.

Chloe smiled back. She wondered what Nando would say if she told him she felt his persistence was part of his charm.

"He's helping the limo driver unload the luggage," she replied. She turned around and called out. "Dalton, darling, come meet our host."

As Chloe watched Dalton walk toward them with his usual loose-hipped grace, she couldn't help but find herself comparing his unconscious casual elegance to Nando's studied continental polish. Both exuded a strong sexual magnetism in their own way. It worried her that Dalton was weaving his spell over her without even trying.

Dalton's white slacks and shirt with the sleeves rolled up his forearms fit his "man without pretension" persona. While Nando, dressed in the same attire, but with a navy blazer and crest stitched on the front pocket and a red scarf tucked in the shirt opening, looked perfect for a luxury cruise.

She suddenly felt underdressed in her black silk pants and sweater with slashed diagonal patterns of fuchsia and black across the front. In deference to the stiff breeze coming off the ocean, she had pulled her hair back in a French braid. She smiled at Dalton as he approached them and held out her hand. He walked up and slid one arm around her waist.

"Nando, I'd like you to meet my husband, Dalton James."

"Signor James, I am very pleased to meet you." He smiled and held out his hand. "You must be very proud of your wife's success."

Dalton flashed her a broad smile as he took Nando's hand. "I'm proud that she's accomplished as much as she has and become so successful all on her own."

Chloe wondered if Nando would feel offended by Dalton's callused palm. One of the first things she had noticed about him years ago was the sandpaper quality of his hands. Not a roughness that irritated but tantalized.

She remained in her place, keeping her smile firmly pasted on her lips as she looked up at the gleaming white yacht docked in front of them.

"It's lovely," she told Nando.

He inclined his head in silent thanks. "Thank you. We use the *Bella* a great deal."

"Maybe we should think about getting one of these, darlin'," Dalton commented, lifting his eyebrows in a comical manner as he grinned at her. "A nice long cruise would be wonderful, don't you think? And if you want to work, we could slip Liza's motion sickness pills in her food."

"My assistant gets seasick just looking at pictures of boats," Chloe explained to Nando, still reeling over Dalton remembering. Unless, her brain reminded her, he'd called Liza and pumped her for information.

"Yes, she had mentioned that to me when I called her with our sailing date and departure," Nando said smoothly. "I'd said it was pity she couldn't join us and she said something about preferring to have her toenails pulled." He shuddered. "Your assistant has a very colorful imagination." He gestured toward the gangway where two young stewards, resplendent in red-and-white uniforms—Bella Skin's colors—stood at attention. "Please, let us get aboard. I will arrange for your luggage to be taken up." He snapped his fingers and spoke to one of the waiting attendants in rapid Italian.

Once they were aboard, he ushered them to the rear of the yacht where a sumptuous buffet was set out.

"I thought we could have a bite of something after we leave the dock," he explained, pouring three glasses of champagne into crystal glasses. "First, we must have a toast to a successful voyage," he suggested, handing each of them a glass. "And to an even more successful alliance between our two companies."

They clinked glasses and drank.

"How large a crew do you carry for a vessel this size, Signor Rossi?" Dalton asked, glancing around.

"Please, call me Nando. After all, we are all friends here. Right now, we have a small crew since there are only the three of us. Only about thirty," he replied.

"Do you just use the yacht for the resort?" Dalton asked.

"Yes. But Bella Skin has two yachts," he proudly announced. "Our other vessel is docked at Capri."

Dalton nodded as if he should have realized that from the beginning. "Of course."

Chloe could have kicked him for the bland expression he adopted. "If you don't mind, I'd like to freshen up a little before we eat," she said.

"Of course." Nando lifted a hand and snapped his fingers. "Maria will show you to your stateroom."

A young woman, so beautiful she could have made even Chloe feel self-conscious, smiled at the couple and gestured for them to follow her.

"I will be your maid for the voyage, *signora*," she explained with a warm smile. "I will unpack and hang up your clothing while you eat."

"Oh, thank you, but I probably won't need your services all that often."

"I've never had a problem in zipping or unzipping my wife's dresses, for that matter," Dalton explained, cupping his hand around the back of Chloe's neck as they walked along. His wicked smile told Chloe he preferred the unzipping part. "Do you work on the yacht full-time, Maria?"

"Yes, I do." Her face lit up with enthusiasm. "I never thought I would have a chance to work on such a lovely yacht." She shot Dalton a shy look bordering on interest. "We always meet very nice people sailing with us."

Chloe slipped her arm through Dalton's as they walked along the deck, then down an inner corridor. She decided if he was going to show a possessive side, she could do the same.

At the end of the corridor, Maria opened double doors and waited for Chloe and Dalton to enter ahead of her.

"Wow," Dalton said under his breath, looking at a stateroom he guessed would rival a suite in any five-star hotel.

As was expected, the rooms were decorated in Bella Skin's colors. The small parlor was outfitted with an elaborate settee upholstered in creamy white with red silk throw pillows. A chair that could easily hold two people was set in one corner with a lamp in the background. A television and electronics system was set into shelves bolted against one wall near an intercom. A collection of bestseller novels, filled a small bookcase. Everything in the room was geared for the guests' comfort. It appeared nothing had been forgotten.

The king-size bed, covered in a red silk comforter, was the first thing Chloe noticed when she stepped inside the stateroom. She breathed a silent sigh of relief when she saw their luxurious room was much larger than she expected. Except once Dalton stepped inside, the room became very cramped.

"It's lovely." She walked around and sneaked a peek inside the bathroom. What she saw in there literally took her breath away.

Lipstick red velvety towels hung on gold racks by the double sinks that were designed to resemble two seashells. The glass shower enclosure was huge while, nearby, black tile steps led up to a round bathtub that looked to have been carved from onyx. The red, black and white color scheme with the gold fixtures only added to the decadence of the room.

Dalton peered inside by looking over Chloe's shoulder. "Now that is what's called a bathroom," he murmured.

Uneasy with him standing so close, she stepped inside and walked over to the tub, pretending to study the bath accessories.

"This is very expensive bath oil," she said, picking up a decanter from a series of glass shelves set in the tile above the tub. She could see, at a glance, the contents offered were everything a woman might desire for her bath. She studied the gold-colored liquid. "Bella Skin sells this for one hundred and fifty dollars an ounce."

Dalton pursed his lips in a silent whistle. "Women will pay that much for bath oil?"

Chloe pulled out the stopper and held the decanter so he could take a whiff. His dark eyes gleamed as he inhaled the exotic fragrance. He straightened up and flashed her another one of his killer grins.

"I think I'd pay double the amount if my woman came out of the tub smelling this sexy. Although, some women don't need perfumed scents to turn on their men."

Chloe almost broke the delicate top as she quickly replaced the stopper on the decanter. Except, even then, the heavy scent lingered in the air between them. The musky fragrance with hints of rare spices, cinnamon and vanilla brought the idea of moonlight spilling across silk sheets to mind. She tamped down on her wayward daydreaming before it got out of hand. She was quickly discovering that, around Dalton, thoughts having to do with sex were dangerous. How many times in the past had he just looked at her and her knees turned to jelly? Even their time apart hadn't lessened his sensual impact on her.

"They cover all the bases, don't they?" Dalton commented, walking over to the mahogany dresser built into the wall and running his hand over the top. He walked over to the electronics cabinet. A variety of videotapes and CDs were stacked next to it. All was identical to the system in the small parlor. "Nothing was spared here for their guests' comfort."

"I think they also want to make sure we're suitably impressed," she replied.

He raised on eyebrow. "Are we suitably impressed?"

Chloe struck an exaggerated model's pose. "We are happy they are working so hard to impress us. That only proves that we know they will be a good company to deal with. Amanda would say the gold bath fixtures are a bit much, but she'd enjoy the decadence at the same time. If Nando thinks all this will soften me up for our talks, he has another think coming. I don't soften easily." She quickly prayed he wouldn't pounce on the last remark. Luckily, he allowed it to pass.

Dalton shook his head. "I guess if the two of you will be busy discussing business, I'll act the part of the spouse and do...whatever."

Chloe walked over to the porthole and looked out. If it hadn't been for the faint shifting motion under her feet, she would have had no idea they were already heading out to sea. She looked over her shoulder. Dalton was already opening his soft-sided travel bag and pulling out his clothing.

"The maid will take care of that," she told him.

He shook his head. "No, thanks, I'd rather do it myself." He picked up a handful of underwear and walked over to the chest of drawers. "Okay if I take this one?" He gestured with his head.

"No problem," she said slowly, trying hard not to stare at the colorful fabric spilling out of his hands.

They were all undeniably skimpy. Her mind loudly demanded to know what happened to his old white briefs. And *who* would give him such wild underwear? Reminding herself that she had no reason to think about this, she quickly turned away, picking up her makeup case and carrying it into the bathroom.

Dalton hid his smile as he gauged the faint look of shock on her face. He had no idea that the presents from his surprise thirty-fifth birthday would come in handy.

While packing for the cruise he'd found the underwear jammed in the back of a drawer and decided bringing them along wouldn't hurt. Not when he recalled Chloe's penchant for silky wisps that passed for lingerie. If they were going to be living in close quarters for a few days he wanted to find out if that kiss outside the restaurant was a fluke. After seeing the way she'd acted from the time she'd picked him up, he had an idea she felt the same *zing* he did.

Now all I have to do is convince her how much better off she was with me, he told himself, taking his time folding and putting away his briefs.

"We should be getting back to Nando," Chloe announced from the bathroom doorway.

Dalton turned and watched her dab perfume on the inside of her wrists and behind her ears. The warm floral scent floated through the air, reaching down to tug at memories. How many times had he enjoyed stroking perfumed oil over her skin?

"I hope that fancy buffet has some real food," he commented, walking over to the door and opening it.

"Knowing Nando, I'm sure he provided everything a person would want," she replied, walking past him.

Dalton dipped his head to murmur in her ear, "But he doesn't have a beautiful wife." He paused, his breath warm against her skin. "Or does he have one hidden away while he roams the world looking for new women to seduce?"

She suddenly feared this wasn't going to work out. The warm scent of his skin tickled her nostrils. "No, he's never married. Why did I let you talk me into using you for this?" she muttered. "I should have told Rachel I wanted someone else. Someone I didn't know."

"Which is exactly why you kept me. Our past meant you didn't have to spend time prepping someone else with all those nitpicky details about you."

He looked so confident she wanted to hit him. That was one of the things Chloe had forgotten about Dalton—his utter self-confidence. Chloe recalled how she envied the way he had easily deflected Amanda's barbs.

She opted to play her queen of the manor role. "There are no nitpicky details about me that would matter."

His breath was warm on her ear as he whispered, "Are you sure about that? How about that you hate peas and cauliflower? Shall we discuss your allergies to plums and peaches, or that you can't sleep without a night-light?"

"I gave that up two years ago," she retorted though gritted teeth, wondering if anyone would notice if Dalton accidentally fell overboard. They weren't very far out yet. He should have no problem swimming back to shore.

He wasn't deterred. "I'll remember that."

When they reached the rear deck, they looked the part of a loving couple to Nando, who sat sipping champagne at a table set under a bright red canopy. He immediately rose to his feet.

"I hope the room is to your satisfaction."

Chloe bestowed a glowing smile on Nando while Dalton's look didn't appear to have the same luminescent quality.

"It's lovely. Thank you. I admit this will be quite a change from flying."

"And much more relaxing than hurrying to and fro, which only adds stress one does not need. We were not meant to rush about so much when we have the ability to take our time and enjoy what life has to offer us." He gestured toward the buffet table. "Please, help yourselves to whatever pleases you."

Chloe's taste buds salivated over the sumptuous feast as she carefully selected her meal. She remained a wary distance from the three-tiered plate of Belgian chocolates.

"We also have a fully equipped gym on board if you wish to work off your meals," Nando announced.

"Sounds good to me," Dalton replied, selecting a little of this and that while keeping a discreet distance from the kippered herrings.

"Do you work out on a regular basis, Dalton?" Nando asked as he assisted Chloe onto her chair. "I admit I cannot see you as a man who enjoys sitting around during the day which is why I was surprised to hear you would be accompanying us. At least, I know the weight room will help you pass the time. We also have a swimming pool and Jacuzzi if you wish to relax."

"I'm more into martial arts than bodybuilding," he explained. "My father taught martial arts while he was in the military, so I started out with that and expanded my knowledge along the way."

"Ah." He nodded. "Did you ever have a chance to visit the Orient?"

"My father was stationed overseas during most of my formative years. I sometimes felt like a masochist as the masters in the art threw me around like a beach ball," he said wryly. "Most days I limped home, wondering if I was going to survive another day."

Chloe kept the look of surprise from her face. While she knew of Dalton's involvement with martial arts, she couldn't remember him ever telling her that the source of his interest had come from his father.

Nando poured them fresh glasses of champagne. Chloe would have preferred something nonalcoholic with her meal. She wanted to keep her wits about her as much as possible.

"I have always been interested in the discipline of martial arts," Nando commented. "Do you also teach it?"

Dalton smiled and shook his head. "No, I never had the patience to take on students. I prefer to spend my time honing my own abilities."

"I am surprised you do not work with Chloe. Especially since the two of you have recently reconciled." He turned and smiled at her as if they were sharing a private joke.

The more Dalton saw of the man's arrogance, the more he decided he didn't like him. But he promised to behave for Chloe's sake. Even if it killed him.

"No, I'm afraid the corporate world isn't my idea of a life." His smile softened his statement. "I'm a sculptor."

Nando burst into a broad smile. "Fascinating. Does a gallery in San Francisco carry your work? I would be interested in viewing it. I always appreciate good art."

"No, it doesn't." Dalton didn't bother to explain that he'd had showings in New York and London the past couple of years. It was fine if Nando wanted to see him as an artist who was still in the struggling phase. He still preferred that Chloe not know of his success just yet. He'd rather find out if there was a chance between them before telling her he wasn't the starving artist she thought he was. Then he'd know she wanted him back because of true love, not because he wasn't the bum Amanda had always accused him of being.

Chloe almost purred as she bit into a large succulent strawberry. Juice squirted its sweet flavor in her mouth. When she noticed the intense expression on Dalton's face, she quickly masked her expression.

"If you do not mind, I suggest we put off any talk about business until tomorrow," Nando brought up. "Today we should relax and enjoy the day. This way, we can talk and get to know each other better." He leaned over in Chloe's direction. "After all, we are going to be working together on merging my skin care with your cosmetics."

It took all of Dalton's willpower not to roll his eyes at the obvious innuendo. Chloe couldn't be falling for this continental line, could she? He watched her closely, but wasn't sure if she was taken in or being merely polite to the man. She wasn't as easy to read as she used to be and he missed that openness she used to display.

He watched her smile. It was the one he always labeled as practiced, not the genuine Chloe he remembered.

At the rate she's going she'll be another Amanda Sumner before the end of the year, he thought, eating but barely tasting the slices of melon he'd selected.

Nando looked from one to the other.

"I must admit, Dalton, that I was surprised to hear you and Chloe had reconciled."

That was enough to start raising his hackles, but he wasn't about to show it.

"Oh?" He gave Nando his best bland smile. Since his host didn't react, it must have been all right. "Any reason why you were surprised?"

He nodded. "It is obvious. Chloe comes from a strong family-business background and you are in the creative-arts field. And I understand you had been divorced for quite some time. It would be natural to assume you would not have reconciled."

"For years it's been known that opposites attract and that's definitely us," Dalton said glibly. "From the first time we met we knew we were meant for each other. Sometimes it takes a long separation for two people to realize that." He flashed Chloe a smile that fairly radiated desire.

"How did you meet?"

Chloe breathed a silent sigh of relief. That was something she might not have thought to inform another hired husband about. Even if she hated to think Dalton was right that she was better off with him. Still, it was daylight now. How was she going to feel about all this when the sun went down?

Dalton reached across the table and took Chloe's hand in his. "We met at Ghiradelli Square." He kept his eyes on her even as he answered Nando's question. "We were in a curio shop that specialized in one-of-a-kind items. We both reached for the same bowl. Neither of us would back down. She accused me of not being a gentleman, and I told her since I was late getting my mother's birthday gift, I wasn't about to be gallant. We ended up tossing a coin. She got the bowl. I got her." He was pleased to see her face color at the sensual twist on his words. This cruise was going to be a success for both of them.

He didn't wince when her nails dug into his skin.

Chloe smiled back. "He makes it sound so easy, but I made sure it wasn't a breeze for him."

Nando burst into laughter, the sound rich and full. "There is nothing more rewarding for a man than to find a spirited woman, is there, Dalton?"

Chloe looked at him, realizing why so many women had fallen for the man over the years. Yet, while he was handsome, charming and wealthy, he didn't stir her as strongly as Dalton did.

Chloe knew if she had ever fallen for Nando's lines and allowed him to make love to her, he would only end up a poor second to Dalton, who could make her body hot just by a certain look.

Her gaze lowered, but she couldn't see anything since the table hid Dalton from the waist down. When he looked at her quizzically, she mustered up a smile.

"It's so lovely out here today," she said brightly, waving her fork for emphasis. "Being at sea makes me want to sail until we reach the other side of the world."

"I'd want to make sure the captain had plenty of fuel first," Dalton muttered, pushing himself away from the table and walking back to the buffet table.

Nando glanced covertly at Dalton's back before leaning toward Chloe, covering her hand with his.

"I understand you had to bring your husband," he murmured in his liquid accent. "After all, your grandmother is a very proper woman and would want these meetings to look aboveboard. Do not worry, we will be sure to make time for ourselves."

Did he mean what she thought he meant? "Time for ourselves?"

He smiled and nodded. "Naturally, Dalton will not be with us when we're talking about the merger, but we will not have to discuss it all the time, will we? After all, we will be on the yacht for several days until we reach the resort."

Now she knew she was in trouble.

"You are very wrong, Nando." She took a deep breath and plunged in. "The only reason we're on this cruise is to begin our discussions for the merger."

He sat back in his chair, looking so supremely male Chloe wanted to hit him.

"Do not worry. We will be discreet, but I know when a woman wants me. And you do." He said the last words with deliberate meaning.

Chloe was stunned. Was the man so egotistical? The way he looked at her as if he imagined her in his bed told her any refusals would be taken as acting coy.

Right now, she was very glad for the protection of Dalton's presence. Because she didn't doubt if she had been alone, Nando would have crept into her stateroom late one night with a bottle of champagne in one hand and two glasses in the other.

"Nando, my husband and I are very happy together," she said in a low voice in hopes Dalton wouldn't overhear. "I wouldn't do anything to jeopardize that."

"Of course you wouldn't," he soothed. "Believe me, my dear, there are ways."

Chloe wouldn't have been surprised if Nando wrote the book on getting around husbands. She wondered how he accomplished any work if he was busy seducing so many women.

"Dalton, darling, would you please bring me another slice of that ham?" she called out.

"Too lazy to get it yourself?"

"Yes."

He forked two slices onto his plate. "All right, but just this once."

Anyone overhearing them would have thought they were just another married couple teasing each other.

Chloe chuckled when Dalton placed the two slices on her plate.

"I figured it would save me a trip," he explained.

She looked up and smiled at him. "Clever man."

He picked up her hand and pressed a kiss in the center of her palm. *This is where you hold my heart.* The words rang loud and clear in her memory. How many times had Dalton told her just that?

Now Chloe felt trapped. What woman wouldn't be if she was stuck on a luxurious yacht with two men trying to seduce her?

Still, Chloe wasn't Amanda's granddaughter for nothing. If anyone was going to win this battle of the sexes, she intended to be the victor.

NANDO PROVED TO BE a charming host as they spent the balance of the afternoon seated on the rear deck, talking about nothing in particular. After they had eaten, they had moved to more comfortable seating. Chloe had chosen one of the chaise lounges where she could stretch out and enjoy the sea air.

She half-listened as Dalton and Nando discussed various art galleries in Venice and Rome they both were familiar with. She was surprised to hear Dalton had spent two years in Europe. But where would he get the money to travel? She closed her eyes, content to let the drone of their voices wash over her.

"Ah, yes, Lucretia." Nando's comment brought her firmly back to earth. "Such a lovely woman. I attended one of her parties just a month ago. She is an excellent hostess, don't you think?"

Chloe opened her eyes just in time to see a light glow in his brown eyes that said he thought of her as more than a hostess. She sneaked a glance at Dalton. Just how well did *he* know the woman?

"Has she finished her sculpture garden for her country home?" Dalton asked.

"Oh, yes. I admit some of the pieces were quite shocking, but they all make you think of her." He chuckled.

Dalton laughed. "Lucretia seems to prefer shocking. She was still busy searching for unique artwork when I was there. The last piece I saw was the threesome." He shook his head. "It definitely left a lasting impression."

Chloe didn't want to admit that for a divorced woman who claimed to have no feelings for her ex-husband she was jealous over talk about another female. Lucretia was probably gorgeous even without makeup. That or she was the type of woman who came to vivid life after dark.

First thing in the morning Chloe always felt pale, and she needed to take time to control the natural curl in her hair and style it into something more becoming the CEO of Chrysalis Cosmetics. She refused to admit her inclination to subdue her natural beauty was because her grandmother had believed her looks were too wild and needed taming.

Dalton hadn't missed the speculation in Chloe's eyes while she looked at him with a deliberately bland expression. He also hadn't missed the tone of Nando's voice. Obviously, he was another one of the sensuous Lucretia's lovers. He remembered the time he had made the mistake of having dinner with her. To this day, he felt as if he had barely escaped with his dignity. He sensed Nando had more than an idea of the erotic art displayed in her bedroom. Now if only Chloe would show a few signs of healthy jealousy!

"Careful, Dalton, or I'll think you weren't pining away the entire time we were apart," she teased, playfully baring her teeth.

Close enough, he decided.

"You were the only one who ever mattered," he soothed her ruffled feathers.

Nando burst into laughter. "I think I am a third wheel here." He rose to his feet. "I will speak to the cook about tonight's menu. Although I allow him to believe he is in charge, I like to play the part of the employer. If there is anything you need, Gino will assist you."

After Nando left them alone, Chloe looked around and noticed one of the stewards hovering a discreet distance away.

"I wasn't sure how the two of you were going to get along at first. At the rate you're going, you will be best friends by the time we reach the resort," she commented, intent on flicking off a piece of invisible lint from her slacks.

"If he's acting like my buddy it's only because he's trying to get into your pants."

"Dalton!" she reproved his blunt words.

He walked over to the chaise lounge and leaned down, effectively trapping her by placing a hand on either side of her shoulders.

"The man wants you, Chloe," he said slowly to better drive in his words. "Every time he looks at you, he sees you in his bed. Were you that afraid of the Italian lothario that you wanted the protection of a husband? And here I thought business always overrode your personal life."

"You're crazy if you think I'd give in to him." Her eyes snapped violet fires.

He smiled, looking as if he didn't believe her, but gentleman enough not to accuse her of lying. Instead, he twisted around and picked up her legs.

He sat down, settling them on his lap. He slipped off her shoes and ran his thumbs across the curves of her insteps. Chloe closed her eyes as tiny shivers ran up her legs.

"Don't stop," she moaned.

"Now that's what I like to hear," he murmured.

Her eyes snapped open and she would have swung her legs down, but he kept a tight grip on her ankles.

"You always did like having your feet rubbed," he commented, continuing to massage them and delving farther up her pants to rub angular circles along her calves. "I couldn't understand why, since it wasn't as if you stood on your feet all day.'' His callused palms rasped against her sheer black stockings. "And then there were the back rubs we used to give each other. Although we did tend to stray from our backs, didn't we?"

Chloe's mind almost exploded with the memories. What started as a back rub never ended as one. This time when she tried to swing her legs down, he allowed it and sat back.

"I have some paperwork I want to look over before tomorrow," she said crisply.

He didn't move when she stood and settled her sweater around her hips with jerky movements. He waited until she started to walk away before he spoke.

"I take it you don't wish to be disturbed while you look over your paperwork," he asked on a sardonic note.

She took a deep breath. "That's right. Thank you for your consideration."

"No problem, Chloe. That's what I'm here for."

As she walked away, she felt as if a minor battle had just been fought. One she lost. And she was well on her way to losing the war, as well.

Chapter Five

Dalton was turned on.

He managed a brief smile as he accepted a glass of wine from Nando. But his eyes were for Chloe.

Dressed in a black silk jumpsuit with a silver-and-black sash belt, she literally sparkled. Dangling silver earrings danced in the air each time she moved her head, sending out faint musical sounds. He wished they were alone.

"Are you sure you wouldn't prefer something stronger?" the man asked, noting his distracted air. "Whiskey?"

Dalton shook his head. "This is fine," he said, lifting the glass to his lips.

"Do you have a special theme you sculpt?" Nando asked, keeping his eyes more on Chloe, who was standing at the railing looking out at sea.

"Many are private commissions." Dalton looked from Chloe to Nando. He had to admit to himself that his host was a likable man even if he did tend to think with his hormones than with his brain at times. Perhaps it was because he was so open with his desires.

Except Dalton knew something Nando didn't. No matter how attracted Chloe might be, she never mixed business and pleasure. Besides, he already sensed there was still a spark left in her soul for him. All Dalton had to do was fan that desire into a flame.

"What kind of commissions?"

"I create statues for business offices or for private collectors," he replied.

Nando smiled. "Erotic art? Are you sure you didn't create something for Lucretia?"

He smiled and shook his head. "Lucretia's requirements were a little more than I was willing to do."

Nando burst into laughter. "Ah, she must have been very disappointed. She once had a lover's, ah, best part encased in plaster, then bronzed so she would have a constant reminder of him. He was very honored to be included in her collection."

Dalton winced even as he wondered if Nando was part of that collection. "That wouldn't be one of my favorite mediums to work with."

"What kind of medium?" Chloe's bright smile bounced between the two men, then slowly faded as she realized they weren't going to let her in on the joke. "Oh, I get it. It's a guy thing, right?" She lifted her glass in a mocking toast.

Nando looked puzzled. "A guy thing?"

"What she means is we were discussing something only another man would understand," he explained.

Nando nodded. "Ah, yes." He lifted his glass in a return toast. "To one of the loveliest ladies I have ever had the pleasure to negotiate with. May all our meetings go as pleasantly as today has."

Chloe smiled her thanks for his compliment. "I enjoy flattery as much as the next woman, but don't think that will mean I'll agree to every one of your terms. I have a few of my own."

"She can be a hard woman, Nando," Dalton spoke up. "Beware of that little-girl face and sweet smile. She's pure steel when it comes to business."

"Is the business what separated the two of you in the beginning?"

Chloe's eyes swept upward to Dalton, but he either pointedly ignored her or didn't notice the slight panic in her gaze.

"I don't think that has anything to do with your talks with Chloe, do you?"

"Call it curiosity," he said. "Indulge me."

He turned and looked at her with something deep and emotional darkening his eyes. "I guess, then, I would say, if anything, I think it was more our not realizing what a good thing we had and cherishing it. Maybe that's the best part about our getting together again. I think we're better off this time because we have the maturity to cherish what we have." He touched his fingertips to his lips and held them out to her for an airborne kiss.

Chloe could have melted to the floor right then and there. She stared at him, stunned by the sincerity ringing in his voice.

She was also mad at herself for feeling upset that it was all an act. She was rapidly learning she wasn't over him, after all.

This isn't going to work out, she thought to herself. *He's acting the part of a loving husband with a little too much enthusiasm.* She took a deep breath.

"You have to excuse Dalton, Nando," she said lightly. "He tends to act like one of those romantic heroes."

"*Cara,* if anyone understands romance, it's an Italian man," he assured her.

Still, she didn't relax until they were seated for dinner. After a wonderful meal of fish, vegetables and pasta, they moved to the salon to listen to music and talk.

This time, it was Dalton who wandered off, pretending to inspect the room's artwork while Chloe and Nando talked in general terms about the merger.

It was an unspoken agreement they wouldn't begin serious discussions until the following day. Chloe thought of the papers in her briefcase—many filled with questions she wanted answered. She had an idea Nando's thoughts were in a similar direction. Although she should have realized he was thinking of ways to get her into his bed.

"WHAT A DAY," Dalton commented as he and Chloe later entered their stateroom. "That guy never stops, does he?"

"Stops what?" She took off her earrings and placed them in her black leather travel jewelry case.

"Trying to seduce you." He dropped onto the bed and fell back, spreading his arms out to the sides. "He must take a lot of vitamin E to keep up all that energy." He stifled a yawn. "I'll tell you this. Business is very tiring."

She glanced in the mirror, watching his reflection as he stretched his arms over his head and arched his back. Every movement of his body seemed orchestrated. And he accused Nando of seducing her! What was he trying to do right now? Oh, he might not be saying the words or touching her, but he was doing it. She already dreaded the moment he would take off his shirt.

"I think I'll take a bath," she announced, opening drawers until she found the one Maria had put her nightgowns in. She pulled one out, went to the closet and drew out her robe. She picked up her book and walked toward the bathroom. She looked over her shoulder. "Would you care to use it first?"

Dalton's smile at her polite question broadened. He scooted along the bed until he lay against the mound of pillows with his arms crossed comfortably behind his head.

"No, you go ahead," he assured her. "I think I'll ask Maria to bring in a bottle of wine. Don't you think it's fitting for our first night at sea?"

Candlelight, wine and a bubble bath. How could she say no to that? She was going to have to remain on her guard twenty-four hours a day. There wasn't any way she would let him think he had a chance in getting to her.

She shot him a dazzling smile.

"If you care for some, feel free to call," she told him as she walked into the bathroom.

The moment the door was closed behind her, Chloe was busy rummaging through her makeup case.

"Where are they?" she muttered, pulling out mascara, eye shadows and blusher. "I put them in here myself."

She calmed the moment the false bottom loosened and she could lift out a plastic bag. She picked one of the chocolates out of the bag and popped it into her mouth.

Her eyes drifted closed as the rich flavors exploded in her mouth. As the chocolate retreated from her taste buds, she thought about a second piece, then reconsidered. She didn't want to run out of them too soon.

Using the running water as a cover, she quickly lit up a cigarette and took several puffs.

"It's a dirty habit," she muttered to herself as she poured bath oil into the water. She took another puff. "A very dirty habit." She took two more puffs, then dropped the last bit of her cigarette into the commode and made sure it flushed away. "I feel much better now."

Chloe shed her clothing and slid into the hot water. She sighed as the warm liquid lapped at her breasts. She cupped bubbles into her palm and playfully blew them into the air. She giggled when they seemed to dance in midair.

She barely had time to react when a knock at the door sounded and Dalton walked in. He held a filled wineglass in each hand.

"Here's your wine."

"What are you doing?" She inched her way down in the water until the bubbles gave her barely adequate coverage.

He couldn't have looked more innocent if he'd tried. Which she greatly feared was his plan.

"Bringing in your wine."

"I didn't ask for any wine."

"You said to go ahead and call Maria, so I did. She brought it and here's yours." He walked over and snagged the red velvet cushioned stool with his leg. He sat down and carefully placed one of the wineglasses on the edge of the tub. The other he kept in his hand. He smiled, looking as if he was going to stay there for a while. "How's your bath?"

She noticed her glares didn't accomplish a thing. "It *was* fine."

He nodded. "Good. Now I think we need to talk."

"About what?"

"About Nando's libido." He sipped his wine. "This is a very good year, but I guess Bella Skin would serve only the best. Try it." He gestured with his glass.

Chloe inched her hand toward her glass and then realized it was set just a little too far out of her reach. The only way she could reach the glass was by leaning forward. A motion she feared would immediately disintegrate the remaining bubbles covering her chest. She managed to keep a smile pasted firmly on her lips.

"Could you hand me my glass, please?" she asked.

Dalton looked from the glass to her. "Are we lazy?"

"No, we are comfortable and don't want to move very far." She started to shift in the water until she realized several bubbles popped. She quickly stilled her movements.

Dalton leaned forward and obligingly slid the glass along the tub edge. If he noticed the creamy fullness of her breasts visible above the iridescent bubbles, he made no mention of it.

"Better?"

"Yes, thank you." She picked up the glass and sipped the liquid. She found it tart and pleasing to the tongue. And just what she needed to help her stay calm. Although she knew the best way for her to relax would involve Dalton's retreat from the bathroom.

"About Nando," he repeated.

"Couldn't we discuss this after my bath? *What are you doing?*"

He calmly ignored her shriek as he leaned over and picked up the sponge lying on the edge of the tub. "I thought I'd wash your back."

"I can do it myself, thank you."

"I doubt you can reach all the tricky places." He dipped the sponge in the water and ran it along her shoulder blades then down in a wide, circular motion.

Chloe closed her eyes against the wealth of emotion overloading her brain. Not to mention memories of baths that started with his washing her back and ended with them almost flooding the bathroom. She swallowed a whimper when the sponge skimmed along the sides of her breasts.

"That's not my back," she said in a strangled voice.

"Sorry." He didn't sound the least bit apologetic as he changed direction, gently rubbing along her spine.

Chloe started thinking about dragging Dalton into the tub with her. She quickly amended that thought. After all, this was a business trip, not pleasure, she reminded herself. Uncaring how she might sound she quickly turned and snatched the sponge out of his hand.

"Thank you, I'm clean," she said primly.

"What's wrong, Chloe? It's not as if I haven't seen you in the bath before. Or naked, for that matter." His mouth curved in a smile that was so sexy it made her toes curl. "We're married, remember?"

"That marriage exists only outside this stateroom," she reminded him. "In here, we are divorced. Which means when I'm in the bathroom, I'm in it alone." She drank her wine, grateful her hand didn't tremble in the least bit.

Dalton didn't appear affronted as he stood. "Don't drown yourself," he advised on his way out of the room.

It wasn't until the door closed that Chloe breathed a sigh of relief. She slid down in the water and rested the back of her head against the edge of the tub.

"How can a man look better every time I see him?"

DALTON DOWNED THE LAST of his wine in one gulp. A decided insult to the expensive vintage, but he needed the numbing effect he hoped would set in within the next five seconds.

Chloe, only wearing bubbles, was a sight to behold—her skin, pink from the steam, curly ringlets of hair falling from her topknot. There had been no way she could tame that wild mane in the steam-filled room.

He closed his eyes and visualized the bubbles covering her pink-tipped nipples. The way the water swirled around her breasts when she picked up her wineglass. For a moment, he seriously thought about diving in the water and recreating some old memories of baths gone by.

He muttered a pithy word as he sat on the bed. He set the glass to one side as he unbuttoned his shirt and pulled it off. His slacks dropped to the floor after his shirt. He wrinkled his nose at the comforter and pushed it to the end of the bed.

"Nothing like spending the night in a floating bordello." He plumped the pillows behind his back as he waited for Chloe to finish her bath. He pulled the tie from his ponytail, ran his fingers through his hair and sat back again. He took a quick glance in the free-standing mirror near the porthole and smiled at his reflection. "This should give her the full effect."

Except Dalton had forgotten Chloe's penchant for long baths. By the time she emerged from the room he was half-asleep. The moment the door opened, steam preceded her out of the room along with the arousing scent of the oil he'd smelled earlier. Except this time, the scent had mixed with her own fragrance, which made it even more arousing.

Dalton sat up, fully awake now.

Chloe hadn't released her hair from its topknot and by now more tendrils had escaped, trailing down her flushed cheeks and nape. Her burgundy plush robe enveloped her slender form, making her look even more petite.

He wondered what she would say if he told her she looked like a teenager with her squeaky-clean face. For a moment she stopped, as if suddenly realizing she wasn't alone in the room.

"I thought you would have been asleep by now," she murmured, walking over to the other side of the bed and placing her book on the small table. Her movements were deliberate, as if she made sure not to look directly at him.

Dalton glanced down at his underwear. Maybe the bright purple briefs with the design of a gold key placed on a significant place was a bit much. He couldn't wait to see her reaction to the pair he had picked out for tomorrow.

"I always find it difficult to settle down the first night in a strange bed," he replied, rolling over onto his side and propping his head up with his hand. "How about you? No, I guess you don't have that problem what with all the traveling you do."

Chloe slipped off her robe and draped it over a nearby chair. She bowed her head, obviously thinking hard before she turned around.

"I think we need to set a few more ground rules here," she stated, looking everywhere but him. Especially at his lower body. "One, while we are presenting a united front outside of this room, there is no reason why we can't have our own space when we're alone."

"Fine. What about two?"

She raised her chin another notch. "I also don't care to hear any more of your opinions about Nando. He is our host and I plan to sign a business deal with him. I don't want you to screw it up."

"Fine."

Chloe used every ounce of willpower not to look at Dalton's body while he was on the bed. His chest and upper arms were more muscled than she remembered with a light smattering of dark hair across the broad contour of lightly tanned skin. She assumed his muscle mass increase was because of his work. She remembered watching him sculpt and was amazed at the sheer power it took to create with clay.

She had hoped if she stayed in the bathroom long enough he would fall asleep.

Except, instead of walking into the room and finding him asleep, he was stretched out on the decadent comforter, looking as if he was her own personal love slave. No man should look this good when wearing a pair of ridiculously skimpy briefs with a picture of a key in a strategic place on his body. And here she thought she felt heated from her bath!

In an effort to keep her wits about her, she said the first thing that came to her mind.

"I was surprised to hear you tell Nando that you'd spent two years in Europe."

"Chloe, we haven't exactly kept in contact with each other since our divorce," he said gently.

She could feel her smile freezing on her face. "You're right. We haven't even talked since then."

His expression darkened. "I tried. You refused."

"It was best for all."

He rolled over until he was more on her side of the bed than his. "Was it?"

Chloe reached up and pulled the clip from her hair, sending the unruly curls tumbling to just above her shoulders.

"There wasn't enough between us to keep a marriage going," she began, sadly thinking of the scant year they'd been married.

Dalton's angry curse stunned her into silence. He straightened up, sitting cross-legged in the middle of the bed.

"You never gave us a try after Dame Amanda told you to dump me. You let her lawyers take over. All I ever got from you was a piece of paper saying you were divorcing me."

She recoiled from his accusation, but refused to retreat.

"Things between us weren't going well even before then and you know it," Chloe argued. "You wanted me to give up my birthright. It was okay for you to demand I give up something I'd worked so hard to achieve. I was looking at an executive position with the company. What were you looking at? More clay to play with?"

Dalton reared back at her painful words. Tight-lipped, he punched the pillow, turned away and moved back over to his side of the bed. Within seconds, he was under the covers.

"I never told you to give up anything. I only asked you to share yourself with me, but I guess that was too much to ask of you," he muttered.

Chloe opened her mouth, fully prepared to apologize for her words, but closed it again. She sensed any apology she might make would be coldly rebuffed. She slipped under the covers and curled up in a tight ball, making sure she remained on her side of the bed.

Feeling as miserable as she did she didn't think she would sleep a wink. Except the events of the day caught up with her and she soon fell into a deep sleep, having no idea that as the night hours passed she and Dalton would instinctively turn to each other until they slept in each other's arms.

And if Chloe had dreams that were more than a little heated it probably had something to do with Dalton's hand warmly cupping her breast as her own arm curved across his waist and one leg nestled intimately between his thighs.

Chapter Six

For once, it didn't take an alarm clock to rouse Chloe from her slumber.

When she opened her eyes, she sleepily took in the elegant room and instantly realized she wasn't in her own bedroom. A tray, holding a silver coffee server, had been placed on the table. The rich aroma of coffee filled her nostrils, bringing her fully awake.

Before she got up, she remained still. Absolute silence. The bathroom door was open and no sounds of occupation came from there. She was alone.

She pulled on her robe and poured herself a cup of coffee. Savoring the rich brew as she sipped, she looked around for an idea of where Dalton would be. Especially when she discovered it was barely 6:00 a.m.

Taking a chance, she crept out of her stateroom. Holding her breath, she made her way down the corridor and along the outside deck until she reached the rear of the ship. It was there she found him.

Although the early-morning air was cool, he wore only a pair of bleached cotton trousers that hung loosely on his hips. Instead of tied back as usual, his hair had been left loose around his face, wisps clinging to his damp cheeks.

She stopped out of sight and watched his graceful movements as he seemed to move to music only he could hear. Each movement his arms and legs made were slow and controlled as if something he had done many times before. As she watched she realized he was doing a form of martial arts. It was like nothing she had seen on television. His bare chest gleamed with sweat as he seemed to almost dance in midair as he leapt upward and kicked out to the side with one leg. There was no doubt if someone had been standing there they would have been taken down with little effort.

Chloe's mouth went dry as she stood and watched him. She had no idea that a man could move so gracefully. That his body could stretch and strain in such a way that reminded her of the times they had made love. Those memories exploded in her thoughts again. The way Dalton concentrated now reminded her of the intensity of their lovemaking. He always had brought her shuddering to the edge until they both fell over into a silken abyss.

She could feel her fingers itching with the idea of touching him. She wanted to run her hands along his shoulders, feel the dampness of his skin. Taste it. She had no idea how long she stood there, out of sight, watching him.

Chloe felt reality rudely intrude on her fantasy.

What was she thinking of? She couldn't just stand there ogling him.

She carefully placed one foot behind her and slowly eased her way backward until she felt safe enough to turn around and almost run back to the stateroom.

When Dalton later walked into the room, she was seated at the table with a cup of coffee and her open briefcase on a nearby chair.

Although she still wore her robe, her hair was brushed back into a twist and her makeup applied. Not by a flicker of an eyelash did she give any indication she had seen him on the rear deck. She looked up and offered him a smile.

"There's plenty of coffee if you wish some?"

Dalton sardonically noticed she used her polite hostess voice.

"No, I think I'll take a shower first." He indicated his sweaty skin. "I'm what you would say less than fresh."

She barely spared him a glance. "Take your time. Nando called and said if we wish to we can meet him in forty minutes in the main salon for breakfast."

Dalton rummaged through the drawers and pulled out fresh clothing. "All right. It won't take me long to get ready." He headed for the bathroom. As he entered he stopped and looked over his shoulder. "You didn't have to remain quiet when you found me out there, Chloe."

Her head snapped up. "You couldn't have known I was there. I wasn't even in view." She then realized that she had just admitted she had seen him.

His lips curved in a smile that could only be described as ironic.

"I didn't have to see you to know you were there," he said quietly. "I've always been able to sense your presence when you were nearby." He offered her a smile that seemed filled with regret before he carefully closed the door.

Chloe sat there, unable to take in his words. She numbly listened to the sound of the shower running...of Dalton naked under steamy water.

She picked up the coffee server and warmed her remaining coffee.

"It's because I haven't dated in a while," she murmured, lifting her cup and sipping the hot brew. "If I had a more active social life, I wouldn't have these strange feelings about him. I'd be just fine. And I wouldn't be wondering what his underwear looks like today."

Then she realized her cup was at eye level. It wasn't the glow of fine bone china shimmering in the morning light she was looking at. It was her hand trembling. She hastily set the cup down before she dropped it.

"Time to get dressed."

Chloe didn't waste any time in pulling out clothing. She decided it wouldn't be a good idea to still be in her robe when Dalton finished in the bathroom.

By the time he walked out, she was dressed in a brick red jumpsuit, the belt secured tightly around her waist. She fumbled with the catch to her necklace, but Dalton merely walked up behind her and secured the clasp. She stilled at the slightly rough feeling of his fingers against her nape.

"Thank you," she murmured.

"My pleasure," he replied, his lips close to her ear. "Might I say you look appropriate for a morning of casual business meetings? Even if your hair does look much better down."

She looked up. "Thank you, but my hair looks more professional when it's worn up."

He placed his hands on her shoulders, making sure she couldn't move away from him too quickly. "Maybe that's why I always preferred it down."

She eyed his jeans. They looked soft to the touch and were a bleached-out color from wear, not because they were made that way. He rolled the sleeves of his white cotton shirt to his elbows.

"With you looking that way, Nando probably won't be able to keep his mind on business and you'll get all the concessions you want," Dalton teased as they left.

"Perhaps you can help by talking more about Letitia with him," she sweetly suggested, walking out ahead of him.

He hid his smile at her deliberate misuse of the woman's name. "Lucretia."

"Whatever."

Nando, looking dapper as ever, sat at the head of the table in the salon. He stood and took Chloe's hand between his.

"*Cara,* lovely as ever." He flashed Dalton a smile. "I trust you both slept well?"

"Just fine," Dalton assured him.

"I worried when I heard you were up early."

He shook his head. "Old habits. I find I do best if I perform my t'ai chi first thing in the morning." He walked over to the serving table and selected a variety of breakfast foods. "Want me to fix a plate for you, Chloe?"

"No, thank you. I think I'll do a little grazing before I decide what I want." She smiled as she walked over to the table.

"Grazing?" Nando questioned Dalton.

"It's turned into a female term for looking over food," he murmured.

She knew she was in trouble the moment her eyes fell on the chocolate croissants. She casually slipped one onto her plate.

"Didn't Dame Amanda once lecture on the evils of chocolate?" Dalton's voice murmured in her ear.

"Put a sock in it, James," she muttered. In penance for the croissant, she also added a variety of fresh fruit on her plate. The idea of her grandmother knowing she was eating chocolate was enough to make sure she didn't go overboard.

"Please feel free to do anything you wish this morning," Nando told Dalton when he sat down.

"I thought I'd make use of your workout room," he replied, using his fork to cut his slice of melon into bite-size pieces.

"I'm sure you will find everything you might require there." He turned to Chloe and asked her a business-related question.

"Why don't we put that on hold until after breakfast," she suggested. "I wouldn't want Dalton bored with our business talk."

Dalton couldn't resist baring his teeth at her. "Dalton is never bored."

"Besides, I'm more interested in this Lucia you spoke of last night," Chloe said with saccharine sweetness.

Nando looked puzzled.

"Lucretia," Dalton said softly.

The other man's face cleared as he now understood. "Ah. Yes, a very lovely woman. And excellent hostess. Her parties in Rome and Venice are legendary," he went on to Chloe. "Several years ago, she decided she wanted to recreate a Roman orgy in place of a birthday party." He chuckled. "She has always had a sense of style when it comes to her parties."

Chloe's smile felt tight on her lips. "Yes, I can gather that."

But he didn't hear her as he went on to further describe the orgy party, complete with bare-breasted slave girls, barely clad men and something that she was certain amounted to a food fight. Except it appeared no one bothered to clean the food off in the traditional manner.

"Only Lucretia could pull off such an outlandish idea," Dalton commented, sneaking sidelong glances at Chloe.

"She visits the resort many times," Nando told Chloe. "Perhaps she'll be there during your visit. I know she would enjoy meeting you."

"I can't wait."

Only Dalton noticed the faint sarcasm in her tone. He quickly finished his meal and stood.

"If you two don't mind, I will leave you to your business talks." He kissed Chloe on the lips and whispered, "Show him your tough side, sweetheart, and he won't have a chance." He inclined his head in Nando's direction before he sauntered out of the salon.

Nando smiled at Chloe. "Shall I ring for fresh coffee before we begin?"

Chloe smiled back. While the Italian had more than his share of lusty thoughts, she also knew the merger would take precedence over his intention to seduce her.

"Let's begin with your idea that your percentage should be increased an additional four percent," she suggested.

WHEN DALTON WALKED into the stateroom after breakfast, he found the bed already made and the coffee tray gone.

"I could use this kind of service at my loft," he murmured, picking up his bag and pulling out a book. He thought he'd read for a while, then head for the workout room. Maybe if he whipped his body into complete exhaustion he could look at Chloe without wanting her so badly even his teeth ached.

He could only wonder if the ten days to two weeks he had would be long enough to prove to her she needed him.

He barely spent an hour with his book before retreating to the workout room. Once inside he was impressed to find it fully equipped. What pleased him the most was the punching bag.

After warming and stretching his muscles, he began practicing his kicks with the bag. Picturing Nando's face on it helped him keep his aim true as he twisted and turned with each kick.

When he finally paused to catch his breath, sweat streamed down his body, but he was barely breathing hard.

"You are very good, Signor James."

Dalton faced Maria, who stood just inside the room. Was it his imagination or had the neckline to her uniform been dramatically lowered?

"It was suggested I see if there is anything you need." She seemed to arch her upper body in an inviting manner.

He would have burst into laughter, but he didn't want to offend the young woman. After all, she was only doing her job. Even if she was willing to take on a few new duties.

"No, Maria, thank you."

"The front upper deck is set up for private sun-bathing if you prefer to be alone," she said in her husky voice that practically oozed sex.

"Thank you." He smiled, but silently indicated she was dismissed. She pouted prettily but left. If nothing, she was well trained.

Dalton shook his head as he walked over to the treadmill.

"This is one cruise I'm glad I didn't miss."

AS THE NEXT FEW DAYS passed, Chloe experienced just how single-minded Nando could be. She learned it took all her wits to keep one step ahead of him as they hammered out details.

Nando shook his head. "No, our evening cream cannot be part of the deal. It is too new on the market."

"And an important part of the Bella Skin product line," she reminded him. "You can't keep it separate and we both know it. Besides, there are a great many women in North America who will want the benefits of that cream." She used her fingernail to trace imaginary lines on the sheet of paper in front of her. "After all, both of us are in the business to make women even more beautiful, right?"

Nando chuckled. "You are using your wiles on me."

"Is it working?"

"I thought you preferred your husband's attentions to mine."

She shook her head, smiling at the intimate tone he affected.

"I realize the adage about catching more flies with honey is appropriate, but don't you think you overdo the Latin lover part just a bit?" she asked. "After all, we're adults here."

"Yes, we are."

She shot him a quelling look. "You know very well what I mean, Nando. I'm happily married. You don't need to try to work your charm on me."

He shook his head. "You don't look happily married."

She attempted a lighthearted laugh. "For someone who isn't married, you seem to enjoy thinking you're an authority."

Nando smiled. "A man doesn't need to be married to know if a woman is well loved."

Chloe opened her mouth to argue that her husband loved her very much. Then closed it just in time as she realized how Nando meant well loved.

"Nando, if you could keep your mind off sex for more than ten minutes you would be a wonderful man," she said, smiling indulgently as if he were a precocious four-year-old. "Now let's finish our discussion about the specialty night cream."

"Discussion, ha!" He threw up his hands. "Every time you insist, I fear I will look into those beautiful amethyst eyes of yours and give in once again."

She playfully batted her eyelashes. "Feel free to give in anytime."

When Dalton, out on the front deck, heard their laughter, he began plotting just how Nando could fall overboard.

THE FAST-PACED THRILLER should have kept her enthralled. But Dalton sprawled in a chair across the room with a sketch pad in his lap was an enticing sight.

Her ex-husband was only wearing a pair of cotton shorts. A man whose lazy movements constantly mesmerized her more than once. She surreptitiously twitched the comforter closer to her neck.

"Good book?"

"What?" She looked up.

Dalton smiled. "Is it a good book?"

Chloe smiled and shrugged, then had to pull the comforter up again to cover her partly bare chest.

"It's great," she lied, although she couldn't remember when she had last turned a page. "Very good."

Dalton's eyebrow arched. "I thought it might be since you had seemed so engrossed in it."

"Oh, yes." She kept her smile firmly pasted on her lips. "Fantastic."

"Then you have better reading skills than I do," he murmured, returning to his sketch pad.

Chloe was confused by his statement until she looked down at her book. And discovered it was upside down. She hastily turned it around, keeping an eye on him as she did so.

"What are you drawing?" She hoped to change the subject.

"I'm working on an idea for a statue for Rachel Harrington's garden," he replied, not looking up as he sketched with quick strokes of charcoal.

"She commissioned a statue from you?" she inquired.

"Not exactly. She has a birthday coming up, so I haven't decided if it will be a surprise for that or if I'll give it to her sooner."

There was no way she could return to her book now. As if she even remembered anything about it. If he was an employed artist, why was he working for Rachel? She decided acting as a husband-for-hire was something he did between commissions. Which had her wondering just how good a friend Rachel was!

"Then you two are good friends?" she verbally probed, ignoring the twinge of jealousy at the idea of the lovely business owner and her ex-husband getting together romantically. Then quickly dismissed it. She couldn't imagine Dalton doing this kind of work and dating his boss.

"We've known each other for quite some time now," he said absently, concentrating on his work.

Why not come right out and ask him, idiot! Chloe silently chastised herself.

"She is lovely," she said brightly, adding under her breath, "Even if she does wear the wrong color of eye shadow."

Dalton looked up with a knowing smile. "What do you want to know, Chloe? If Rachel and I are, or ever have been, lovers?"

"Naturally not!" she haughtily declared. "Your love life is none of my business."

"But that doesn't stop you asking, does it?" He set his sketch pad and pencil on the table beside him and stood.

For a moment, all Chloe could see was the sinewy length of man. With the time he had spent outdoors the past few days his skin had darkened to a light bronze and she even thought she could detect gold highlights in his dark hair, which now hung loosely around his shoulders.

Each morning, she sensed his absence the moment he crept out of bed, pulled on the loose cotton pants and went outside to meditate and perform his exercises.

She was only grateful she had been able to remain on her side of the bed as she slept. If she instinctively had gone to him in her sleep, she would have been horrified.

As it was, playing the part of the loving wife was proving to be a lot of wear and tear on her nerves. It wasn't just her role for Nando that left her feeling frazzled. It was the hours she and Dalton spent alone in the stateroom....

For now, she was watching him with a wary gaze as he walked toward the bed. With each shift of his body, she was made aware of the prime male specimen before her.

"Are you finished with your sketch?" She kept her gaze on his knee, which was resting on the end of the bed.

He glanced back at the table, then turned back to her.

"No."

She felt her throat suddenly turn dry. She coughed quietly to relieve it. "Having trouble coming up with an idea?" She was determined to keep this as light as possible. Except he was getting closer by the second as he crawled up the bed on his knees.

"Not at all." He stopped when he was in front of her drawn-up knees. He placed a hand on each knee and slowly leaned forward.

She was positive the heat from his hands was melting the silk fabric until only her dark green soft cotton nightshirt would be between him and her.

"Dare I ask what you're doing?" she inquired in a hushed tone.

He tipped his head to one side and lowered it another fraction of an inch.

"Let's call it a test," he murmured.

She couldn't take her eyes off his face. There was a faint roughness to his skin since he hadn't shaved before dinner tonight.

And his lips, that beautiful mouth that used to do such wonderful and delicious things to her, was very tempting and very close. No man could kiss the way he could.

She suddenly remembered how he would take his time kissing her so thoroughly she thought she would go insane. She was hungry to experience those mind-stealing kisses again.

"What are we testing?" Her voice grew husky with memories.

His mouth lowered that last fraction of an inch. "I want to see if the magic is still there," he murmured just before his mouth covered hers.

The moment his lips touched hers, Chloe knew the magic was most definitely still there.

Firm, warm, slightly moist, his lips partially opened while his tongue seduced its way inside. As if there would have been any argument on her part. By now, she was past protesting. Chloe knew she couldn't blame it on misplaced hormones or being alone for so long. It was all Dalton. Only he could make her feel this way.

She curved her arms around his shoulders, feeling the heat of his skin against hers as she slowly slid down the bed with him following her down. The comforter slid to one side as they rolled to the middle of the bed with Dalton's body fully over hers.

His knee nudged her legs apart as he settled himself in the cradle of her thighs. And all the time his mouth never left hers. She inhaled the exotic honey almond smell on his skin. A scent she'd never forgotten over the years because she had always associated it with him.

His mouth slid along her jawline until it reached her ear. He nibbled on her earlobe and exhaled a soft breath into the curved interior. Then murmured a few sexy words that brought a soft moan to her lips as she visualized the scene he described so potently.

From past experience Chloe knew Dalton had an incredible imagination and he had always been more than willing to use it when it came to their lovemaking. He was so inventive he could even make her believe they could make love on another planet. Right now, she wouldn't care if they were in the middle of the Golden Gate Bridge just as long as he didn't stop.

For the moment, she preferred to concentrate on the enchantment he wove around them. She could feel her nipples tighten almost painfully with her arousal as his chest brushed against her breasts.

She moaned softly into his open mouth, shifting under his pleasurable weight as he covered her with his body. There was no rushing him. She knew he always took his time and, obviously, this wasn't going to be any different. She gently raked her teeth over his chin, feeling the delicious abrasion of his beard against her skin.

"It hasn't changed, has it, Chloe?" he murmured, weaving his fingers through her hair and gently drawing her head back so that her neck gracefully arched. "We can still ignite each other in seconds. Right now, I'm so hot for you I feel as if I could go up in flames in seconds. No one could ever excite me the way you could just by looking at me with those witch's eyes of yours."

She had no doubt of that. All she had to do was feel the hard ridge of desire pulsating against her thigh.

She moved under him, sensing her body softening and liquefying in preparation for his possession. Her body recalled what her mind didn't want to. And once her body remembered, the memories crept into her mind, sending tantalizing visions across the surface of her closed eyelids.

"Talk like that could get us both in trouble," she whispered, running her fingers along the slope of his shoulders. His skin felt hot and smooth against her fingertips. She wanted to touch him all over, to see if her memories were true. She had an idea the fantasy would be exactly the same as the truth.

He ground his hips against hers. "Are you willing to get into that kind of trouble, Chloe?" His black eyes bored into hers, silently demanding she tell the truth. "Are you willing to take a chance and tell the world to go to hell?"

Her breath caught as she realized the significance of his words. He was asking for more than their making love that night. He was asking for forever.

Don't worry about it, darling. The Sumner women have much better luck in business than they do with love. That's where our rewards are, Amanda had told her the day her divorce became final and she had cried until she was almost ill because all she wanted was Dalton back. *Your grandfather couldn't handle it, your father refused to and, well, I'm afraid you're part of our curse. But you're not to worry. Someday, an appropriate man will appear and you'll have a child to carry on the business.*

The moment her body stiffened, Dalton knew her answer. He mentally cursed Amanda Sumner because he knew the woman had to have something to do with it. He levered himself off her and sat back, showing no inclination to hide his arousal.

"So tell me, what warning did Dame Amanda offer you before you took this cruise?" he asked with a sardonic smile. "Did she tell you to make sure your artsy ex-husband keep his clay-covered hands off you? She wouldn't want you to make another mistake, would she? You know, I would think she would have picked out a suitable candidate for you." He suddenly snapped his fingers. "Wait a minute, I forgot, she doesn't approve of men in your life, does she? They might want their piece of Chrysalis." His dark gaze speared her with a painful intensity. "All I ever cared about was you. All my love for you ever got me was a divorce decree."

She pulled the comforter over her. She felt naked, although not even a button had been released from her nightshirt. As it was, she felt as if her entire body prickled with unfulfilled desire. Every nerve ending was on fire.

She wasn't sure whether to hate herself for allowing the situation to get out of hand or for allowing Amanda's too-sane voice to intrude.

The last person she would blame was Dalton since she had certainly invited his attention. And right now, she wouldn't mind dragging him back to her so he could finish what he started.

But she wasn't sure she could look at him as she quietly admitted, "She doesn't know you're here with me."

He wasn't sure he heard correctly. "What?"

Chloe looked up with eyes snapping with anger. "You heard me. Amanda doesn't know you're with me."

His mouth, still moist from their kisses, curved upward. "So she trusted you while you didn't trust yourself. How interesting." He pushed himself off the bed.

"What are you doing?" She hoped he wasn't going to blow things by demanding a separate stateroom. Seeing the dangerous look in his eye, she wasn't sure what to expect.

Dalton pulled underwear out of the drawer. This pair was bright red with candy canes scattered all over it.

"I am doing the only thing a husband would do in this kind of situation. The one action that would keep him reasonably sane," he said as he walked into the bathroom. "I'm going to take a very long and very cold shower."

She waited until the door closed before she murmured, "Don't use all the cold water."

Chapter Seven

Their truce became a fragile one. Every time Dalton smiled or kissed her when Nando was around, Chloe felt as if she had been burned.

The hypocrisy was eating away at her like acid and she was afraid it was affecting her mental processes. The pages of the agreement she and Nando had finished were pitifully few because she couldn't keep her mind on the merger.

"How's it going?" Liza asked during one of Chloe's twice daily calls to the office. Because the afternoon meeting had run over after a three-hour argument over a percentage on one of the creams, Chloe had called her assistant at home to give her the update.

She grimaced. "It could be better."

"Better? Boss lady, you have the chance of a lifetime. You're on a yacht with two gorgeous men who no woman in her right mind would kick out of bed. You know, some of us single women would kill for that kind of opportunity."

"The yacht has a helicopter pad. Come out anytime. I'll even let you choose which one you want."

"No, thanks. I'd only ruin the effect by constantly throwing up. Besides, someone has to protect Brenda."

Chloe closed her eyes. She was afraid to hear, but couldn't stop herself from asking. "Do I want to know what happened?"

"Probably not, but it's not as bad as you think. Amanda was in yesterday. She checked the progress reports you sent in and then announced she was taking Brenda to lunch. Brenda protested she had a lot of work to do, but you know that never stops Amanda. She told Brenda she likes to get to know all the new employees and her retirement from active work hasn't stopped her from doing that. In short, she reminded Brenda she still had some power around here."

"She has always been good at that," Chloe murmured. "Poor Brenda never had a chance. How long were they gone?"

"They returned three hours later," Liza went on. "Brenda now has a new hairstyle and a complete make-over. She told me Amanda took her in for the works. She had a facial, manicure, pedicure and massage. I told her not to worry and let Amanda pamper her. She does these things every so often as a reward."

"Amanda does it because she feels it's another way to remain in control," Chloe retorted.

"That, too. But I didn't have the heart to tell her that."

Chloe looked up as she heard the door open and close. Dalton walked in, glanced at her and went over to a corner of the room, picking up a magazine along the way.

"Anything else going on I should know about?" she asked in a crisp tone.

"Oh, my, we've put on our Madam CEO mask. Did that sexy husband of yours just walk in?" Liza's voice turned sly.

"What about marketing? Did they get their month-end report in?"

"I was right, he's there. Come on, give me something to think about," she begged. "Does he still have that sexy body? I swear, the man always looked as good clothed as I imagine he looks naked."

"You are sick," she hissed into the receiver, turning away from Dalton.

"No, just having a lousy love life, so I figure if yours spices up I'll have something to think about. Although, I would say mine is usually better than yours has been in a long time. Come on, tell all. Does he still look good?"

Chloe didn't have to turn around to know Dalton was watching her.

"Yes," she finally admitted.

"Aha! If you've noticed that, you're on your way! Ask Nando if he'd be willing to give up the yacht for me and I'll help him choose a lovely corporate jet. You can't be greedy, Chloe. You've already got Dalton, so you don't need Nando, too. I'll even sign up for Italian lessons."

"Liza!"

She was unfazed by her boss's shock. "Now come on, Chloe, you can't tell me you haven't thought of getting Dalton back full time. The two of you were a perfect match back then. I can't imagine things have changed that much. He doesn't have a girlfriend, does he?"

Chloe froze, then just as quickly relaxed. If Dalton had a woman in his life, he wouldn't have agreed to accompany her on the cruise. Not only that, but he definitely wouldn't have kissed her. They might have had their differences in the past, but she could never fault his personal code of honor. First and foremost, Dalton James was a gentleman. He would never dishonor a woman he was involved with.

"No," she said firmly. "There is no reason for it."

"What I wouldn't give to be a fly on the wall out there," Liza teased.

"I'll have to check my calendar. I'm sure your review is coming up soon."

The woman laughed, not the least bit afraid of her boss's implied threat. "Sounds good to me. I'm due for a big raise. Especially with my keeping everything in order here while you're sailing the Pacific with two gorgeous men."

"Don't worry, I'll take you with me next time and we'll leave the Dramamine home." With that, Chloe hung up and settled back in her chair.

"Wow! What did Liza do to tick you off?" Dalton put his magazine to one side.

"Not a thing."

"Is that why you're grinding your teeth? Not a good idea, you know."

Hating to admit he was right, she relaxed her jaw. "I'm sorry if this cruise is proving to be boring for you."

"I haven't been bored at all," he replied. "Nando plays a pretty good game of eight ball and, for once, I've had time to work on sketches."

"Do you still concentrate on people or do you create abstracts?"

He was heartened to hear her expressing interest in his work.

"With private commissions I do a little of each, although I still prefer to work with abstracts. Most of the time the client tells me what they want, I work up a few sketches and we go from there," he explained.

Her lips curved. "Any 'private' commissions for Louise?"

He grinned back. "You love to deliberately call her the wrong name, don't you?"

"Any woman who asks that her lover's genitals be encased in plaster so she can enjoy the memories deserves a lot more than being called the wrong name," she retorted, raising one leg and curling it under her so she could sit on it.

"She has her moments."

"Did you make love to her?"

Dalton waited for Chloe to realize how personal her question was and retract it. The old Chloe would have backed up with rapid murmurs of embarrassed apology. The new Chloe looked at him squarely, patiently waiting for his answer.

"What would you do if I said yes?"

"Inform you that you will not sleep in that bed again until you've had a blood test," she said without hesitation. "I'd hate to think you've picked up anything nasty. Although, in this day and age, I would hope one of you took the proper precautions."

"I'm sure she always did. She is a beautiful woman and very sexy, but not my type."

She lifted an eyebrow. "Oh? And what is your type?"

With her head thrown back, her features were highlighted by the lamplight coming down behind her.

She looked beautiful and elegant even in the scruffy shorts and tank top she had on. Dalton wondered what prompted her to bring such a disreputable outfit with her. When she wore them, she refused to step outside of the cabin. He looked up at the ceiling as if pondering her question, then looked across the room at her.

"My wants are few. Someone intelligent. Well read. Eyes that aren't afraid of revealing the soul. A bit of a temper would be nice. I don't want anyone passive who will say yes to everything I ask. Someone who's willing to pitch in when things are rough. Not financially but emotionally. Someone who's there. No matter what."

There was no telling how long the silent battle would have gone on if he hadn't suddenly broken eye contact by getting up. He stretched his arms over his head and arched his back.

"You know, a swim sounds good about now. Want to come?" He smiled disarmingly as if the tension between them a few seconds ago hadn't almost risen to the boiling point.

Chloe immediately thought of drowning him. Then she remembered the swimming pool and spa the yacht boasted. But she envisioned Dalton swimming laps in that bare excuse he called swim briefs. She dredged up a smile.

"No, I think I'll finish going over these papers." She held up the paperwork she was using for her excuse. "Have fun."

He walked over and leaned closer, fencing her in with his hands placed on the chair arms.

"I'd have more fun if you were going swimming with me," he said quietly. "Or you could relax in the spa."

The idea of heat-bubbling water relaxing her tense muscles was tempting.

"You won't expect me to swim laps?"

He solemnly shook his head.

"And I'll have the spa all to myself?"

Just as seriously he nodded.

She planted her hands on his chest and pushed him backward so she could get up. "Give me five minutes."

Dalton changed in the bedroom while Chloe used the bathroom. When she came out, she wore a cotton cover-up over her suit and had pulled her hair up into a ponytail that bounced against her nape.

"Once you see the pool you're going to want to swim laps," he assured her as they walked to an upper deck. "It's too bad you haven't taken advantage of it before."

"I don't swim laps," she argued.

Dalton walked over to a chest and pulled out two towels. He handed one to her. "You used to."

"Only because you used to trick me into racing you. That stunt won't work again."

When they reached the swimming area, she pulled her cover-up over her head and placed it on a nearby chaise lounge. Dalton drew off his shirt and immediately dove into the pool. With swift strokes, he reached the other end in record time.

Chloe had to smile at his display of strength.

"Show off," she muttered, walking over to the spa and setting the controls. She waited for the water to begin bubbling before she dipped her toes in. Finding it already pleasantly warm, she quickly lowered herself in the water.

Chloe rolled her towel and stuck it behind her neck as she sat in front of one of the jets so the stream of heated water could ease the tightness in her back. She looked up at the dark sky, admiring the many stars overhead.

"This is the life." Her words ended on a breathy sigh.

A hint of a splash caught her attention. She opened her eyes and watched the lean figure slicing as if jet propelled through the water from one end of the pool to the other. The only lights on were the ones illuminating the pool's interior.

"No one should look that good," she murmured.

"Ah, *signora*." Maria appeared just above her. "I did not realize you were out here with Signor James."

Chloe's smile felt a little stiff. Every time she saw the maid her neckline appeared to be lower.

"Would you care for anything, *signora?*" the maid asked, shifting uneasily under Chloe's knowing look.

"A wine spritzer, light on the wine," she replied, then raised her voice. "Dalton, sweetie, would you like something to drink?"

He swam over to the side and braced his arms on the coping. He shook his head to toss the wet hair from his eyes. He flashed a grin at Maria.

"Whatever my wife is having is fine with me."

"Wine spritzer?" Chloe asked.

He nodded. "Maria, maybe you could put it in a pitcher so we could help ourselves?" he suggested. "That way we wouldn't have to bother you for refills."

"You never bother me, signor." Her expression would have been coy if it hadn't been for the heat in her brown eyes.

"Yes, but that way we can be assured of privacy."

She inclined her head, although she couldn't quite hide her disappointment.

"Of course."

"Dalton, you bad boy, you hurt her feelings," Chloe teased once she knew the maid was out of earshot. "She was hoping for the chance to give you a bit more personal assistance."

He rolled his eyes, then looked around. He didn't want anyone overhearing him, either. "The woman is a regular barracuda. I'm surprised I still have my virtue intact."

"*Ha!* You lost your virtue years ago."

"Virtue, my love, not virginity."

Chloe stared across the space separating them.

"We couldn't have had this conversation years ago, could we?" she asked in the hushed silence.

"Not politely," he admitted. "There was always too much between us."

Chloe stood, aware of the water streaming down her body. She walked up the steps and over to the pool. She dove in and swam over to Dalton. She quickly discovered she had to tread water. Something she felt she had been doing from the beginning.

"I've decided you're more dangerous than Nando ever could have been," she said quietly.

He turned around, stretching his arms along the coping.

"Any reason why?"

"You know why." Several emotions flared in her eyes—desire mingled with confusion with a touch of regret. The amethyst color deepened as she stared at him.

He sensed this was the best time for him to get a few true answers.

"Why did you leave me, Chloe? Everything was so good between us."

She smiled, but there was no laughter or humor, only sorrow. "Because the Sumner women can't have a home and family when there's Chrysalis to run."

He opened his mouth, fully intending to find out exactly what she meant when the maid returned.

"Here are your wine spritzers," Maria announced, placing a tray holding a pitcher and two glasses on a nearby table. She glanced from the spa to the pool. Her expression told them she sensed she was interrupting something important. "I also brought out some hors d'oeuvres in case you wish something to eat."

Dalton was the one to recover first. "Thank you, Maria. Is it possible for us to be left undisturbed?"

"Of course."

The moment she walked through the main salon, Dalton turned back to Chloe. The expression on her face told him the moment was lost. There wouldn't be any more confessions that night.

"How many laps can you manage?"

She looked relieved he wasn't going to press her for any more answers.

"Without dying?"

He nodded.

"There's no way I can keep up with you."

"I remember a lot of times you kept up with me just fine."

Chloe's face burned.

"Why do you have to turn every conversation we have into something sexual?" she blurted out.

His eyes dropped, seeming to burn their way through the water to better see the bright red bikini she wore. The top's sweetheart neckline revealed the lovely curve of her breasts while the slight V cutout in her waistband revealed the smooth lines of her hips.

Without even thinking about it, he quickly reached out and grabbed hold of her. She muffled her shriek against his shoulder as she flung her arms around his neck. It took her only a couple seconds to realize if it wasn't for his legs easily treading water they would have gone down.

"Hang on tight, baby, if you don't want to drown," he told her with a grin. His fingers fanned out over her torso, several dipping below her bottom's waistband.

"Not funny, Dalton." She gasped, then jumped again when she realized his wandering fingers were traveling more south than she expected.

"You know what it is about you that makes me hot?" he told her while nibbling on her ear.

She found it hard to breathe. "What?"

"You always look so cool and composed. So untouchable," he murmured, continuing his sensual feast. "The first time I saw you, I thought of Elizabeth Taylor when she played her lady of the manor roles. You were always impeccably dressed, your hair brushed into those touch-me-not twists and made up to look like a fashion model." He brushed her hair from her eyes, then returned to stroking her torso just under her breasts. "You're a temptation, Chloe Sumner. You make me want to mess you up a little. See you with your clothes all rumpled, your hair all wild and curly." He punctuated each whispered word with a kiss against the tip of her nose and corners of her mouth. "Smear your lipstick." He breathed in the faint chlorine odor overlying her own scent. "I always liked to listen to you moan as you shivered around me. Nothing ever turned me on faster than your responses." His fingers brushed the soft hair at the delta of her thighs. "Remember how it felt between us?"

A soft moan left her lips as she listened to the words that painted pictures of the past. She didn't think twice as she twined her legs around his waist, feeling his erection. Her mouth melted under his as he ground his lips against hers.

Chloe remembered Dalton's kisses the past few days and none held the heat and passion that this one did. He held nothing back as he made love to her with his mouth. His grip tightened as their kiss intensified. He muttered a curse as he tried to push her bikini bottom off while she fumbled with his briefs.

They were so intent on their needs that they didn't think of their precarious location. This time Chloe's shriek wasn't muffled as she grabbed hold of Dalton's shoulders as they both slipped underwater. She bobbed up, coughing.

Chloe swam back to the shallow end and sat on the steps. Dalton followed her.

She wasn't sure whether it was the wry expression on his face or the way he just sprawled on the steps. She hid her face in her hands.

"I'm sorry, Chloe," he murmured, touching her arm with his fingertips. "I should have remembered we were in danger of drowning. Please don't be upset." He grew alarmed when he noticed her shoulders shaking. "Chloe? Are you all right?" His voice sharpened.

She lifted her head, unable to stop her laughter from spilling out.

"Talk about a headline for the *Wall Street Journal*," she giggled. "Cosmetics CEO Drowns While In Compromising Position." She burst into laughter again, laughing so hard she lay back in the water. "What would Nando have thought if he came looking for us?"

Relieved she wasn't angry, Dalton couldn't help but join her.

"So you're not mad at me for taking advantage of the situation?"

She shook her head as she climbed out of the pool. She wrapped a towel around her body and sat down, filling the two glasses with wine spritzers.

"I wanted it as much as you did," she told him. "But I also know our carrying it through would have only made matters worse. Fate is telling us to keep things on a friendly basis. I'd like to know we can continue that friendship when we return to San Francisco."

For a moment she thought he wasn't going to answer her.

"I'd like that, too."

If that was what she wanted to hear, why did she feel a strange sense of loss at his reply?

"YOU ARE A VERY hard woman," Nando announced.

Chloe sat back with a satisfied smile. "You're only calling me difficult because I'm winning all our disagreements."

He shook his head, clearly disgruntled with himself.

"I call you difficult because you make too much sense. The women in our company do not have the smarts you do. What would it take to lure you away from Chrysalis?"

She laughed. "Nothing you offer would tempt me. Besides, then you would have my grandmother to contend with."

He nodded. "Signora Amanda. She is a formidable woman." He leaned back his chair and rolled his fountain pen between his fingers. "I will be honest with you, Chloe. If Bella Skin's board of directors had known exactly what kind of woman Amanda was, they might have reconsidered her offer."

"Be honest, Nando. After your people heard our offer, you immediately had us thoroughly investigated just as we had you. After you learned how fast we've grown in the past two years and we found you needed a new client base—it was a match made in heaven."

"You will have many advantages, also. After all, our people will be selling your cosmetics in our spas," he reminded her.

"Which makes us both benefit."

"Ah, but we've given you our special night cream."

Chloe leaned over the table. "But, Nando," she lowered her voice to a husky purr, "I want much more. I'm greedy."

If he hadn't noticed the wicked twinkle in her eyes he would have hoped for another kind of greed.

"You are a very naughty woman," he chided.

Chloe would have burst into laughter if Dalton hadn't walked into the salon at that moment and heard the last few sentences.

"Hi, sweetheart," she greeted him with a broad smile.

He didn't return her smile. "Sorry if I disturbed you," he said stiffly, rapidly backing out.

"You're not!" her protest was ignored as he walked away.

Nando lifted an eyebrow. "I think I detected a hint of jealousy."

"Dalton, jealous? We weren't doing anything that would cause him to get upset. Besides, he's not the jealous type," she assured him.

"I have observed the way your husband watches you when we are together," he said casually. "I think he would be happier if you dealt with a woman."

She concentrated on the papers in front of her. "I suggest we get back to business."

"He watches you with hungry eyes."

Chloe lifted her face. "Leave it, Nando."

He threw up his hands. "I'm Italian. Love is my business. I have also seen him do his martial arts first thing in the morning. I would think a man who is enjoying a romantic cruise with his wife would be too tired to get up so early."

"Dalton has always meditated and practiced his movements in the morning," she said hastily. "He feels it helps him focus for the rest of the day."

Nando merely smiled. "We will be arriving at the resort tomorrow. Perhaps we can find him other ways to focus where you will not always have your mind on business and have more of it on him." He glanced at his watch. "I have a few calls to make now. I especially need to tell my superiors that a few numbers will be changed. I only hope they will understand.''

"You haven't lost all the battles," she reminded him. "If I recall correctly, a few of those numbers will be changed in your favor."

He smiled. "Yes, but I hoped to make you feel guilty, so you would offer to comfort me. Obviously, it did not work."

She rose from the table. "Not at all."

Chloe walked back to the stateroom in hopes of finding Dalton there. Since the night in the pool, their relationship had taken another change. Evenings were spent with Nando. The men either played pool with outlandish bets or the three of them talked.

Except Chloe realized that Nando seemed to have done most of the talking, which meant she learned very little about Dalton. He would mention points of interest in Europe, but he didn't reveal any tidbits of his life during the past six years.

She made a mental vow to make time for them to be alone and seriously talk while at the resort. After all, her and Nando's negotiations were almost over.

At the back of her mind was even the idea they could get together once in a while for dinner when they returned to San Francisco. She immediately thought of her grandmother's reaction to her seeing her ex-husband again. This time, Chloe didn't care what Amanda said. She knew she couldn't have an intimate relationship with Dalton. The family curse took care of that. But she saw no reason why she couldn't remain friends with him. If she thought about him seeing other women and how it would make her feel, she preferred to keep the knowledge hidden deep down within her soul.

Dalton wasn't in their room, and by the time he arrived, it was time for them to meet Nando for dinner.

"Where were you?" she asked him as she fastened a silver filigree bracelet.

"Talking to some of the staff," he said tight-lipped. "Is that all right?"

She didn't miss his silent challenge. "Of course."

He turned away as he pulled clothing out. "You were busy. I found a way to keep myself out of trouble."

She couldn't help but notice the bright green briefs he chose. And thought how they would look on his lean hips.

It was a crime for a man to look so good, she thought to herself.

"I'll meet you in the dining salon," she murmured, guessing the air might clear if she didn't ask him any more questions just now.

"Right."

Except dinner went from bad to worse. Dalton said little and even Nando realized something was very wrong.

"You must be very proud of your wife," Nando said as they enjoyed after-dinner coffee and brandy. "I have never met another woman with the incredible business knowledge she has."

Dalton's eyes glittered with dark lights as he stared at her from across the table. Tonight, he'd worn a black shirt and black pants, which was most appropriate for his grim mood. "She does have her good points." He turned back to Nando. "But then I'm sure you already know that."

"Dalton!" She was stunned by his implication.

He upended the balloon glass for no regard to the fine brandy he just swallowed and stood.

"If you two don't mind, I think I'll take a stroll around the deck." He offered a mocking smile to Nando. "I'm sure I can trust you to entertain my wife."

Chloe was positive her face burned a bright red as she watched him walk out of the salon.

"I'd like to apologize for him," she said unsteadily.

"Why? For speaking the truth." He seemed to look delighted with the scene that just unfolded. "My dear, I enjoy watching a man who is clearly in love with his wife. It makes me believe there is a woman out there for me." He stood and lifted her hand to his lips. "Go find your man and lure him back to your cabin," he advised. "After all, tomorrow he will be surrounded by many women at the island. Show him you are the only one that matters."

Chloe thought of taking part of Nando's advice— finding Dalton. Except she didn't locate him.

In the end, she settled in bed alone, and even though she thought her anger would keep her awake, it wasn't to be. She finally fell into an exhausted sleep.

Her fitful sleep was disturbed by the sound of the door opening. She sat up in bed, relieved to see Dalton walk in. As he crossed through the parlor into the bedroom she realized he wasn't walking all that straight and the strong smell of wine entered the room with him.

"Ah, my loving wife," he mocked, sketching a bow. "I'm crushed. You didn't wait up for me."

"You're drunk."

He laughed at her accusation. "I can't get drunk. Don't you know that?" He pulled off his shirt and tossed it on a chair. "Besides, I thought you would have preferred to be alone with Nando. We all know he wants you. Maybe you decided it was easier to seal a deal that way than with a handshake."

She shot out of bed as if propelled by a cannon. As she crossed the room, murder was heavy on her mind. Even inebriated, Dalton's reflexes were much faster than hers. He grasped her wrist and pulled her to him.

"You've always been mine, Chloe," he said in a rough, compelling voice as he lowered his face to hers. "Remember that."

"The last thing I want to hear from you is a Neanderthal statement like that." She pulled free, although deep down she knew she wouldn't have been able to go if he hadn't allowed it. "Go take a cold shower and sober up. Then we'll talk."

"What do you think I've been doing all these nights?"

With his thoughts so clearly echoing hers, since cold showers had become a part of her daily habit, too, she knew she had to get away. Without bothering with a robe, she stalked out of the room. It took a moment for him to realize what she was doing and was quickly on her heels.

"Where are you going?"

"Anywhere you're not," she snapped back, walking toward the rear deck. She was grateful no one was about to see her parading around in her pajamas. While the cobalt blue tank top and ankle length bottoms were cut for comfort, they still weren't meant for public viewing.

"Oh, no. You started this fight, you're going to finish it." He grabbed her arm and twirled her around.

"You're the one who's been acting like an idiot all evening," she accused.

"I don't like Nando inferring you two are on the verge of a hot and heavy affair."

"That's the last thing that will happen!" She pushed him back and walked toward the railing. She stared at the black waves below, feeling as if the angry water imitated her own turmoil.

Dalton advanced on her. "Not if he has anything to say about it."

"Spare me the jealous bit. It doesn't suit you!"

"How do you know what suits me?" He started to reach out for her again, but she pushed him away and stepped to one side at the same time.

Neither knew what happened then. The yacht turned one way and Chloe turned the other. Before she could regain her balance, her foot slipped out from under her and she fell against the railing and slipped over it. Her terrified scream was swallowed up by the muted roar of the yacht's engines. All she remembered was hearing Dalton shout her name as she hit the water with a painful thud and her world went black.

Chapter Eight

Chloe was hazily aware of a bright light seeming to sear the back of her eyes. Then she felt a dryness in her throat and pain radiating all through her body. When she opened her eyes a slit, she realized she was lying in a pair of arms and a man's voice was begging her to open her eyes.

"I hope you got the number of the truck that hit me," she croaked, struggling to sit up. "Because I plan to sue."

Dalton's body grew limp with relief. He pulled her against his chest, wrapping his arms around her in a tight grip.

"Thank God," he murmured.

"Dalton." His name came out on a wheeze. "Dalton." He only hugged her harder. "Dalton, I can't breathe."

He instantly released her and sat back on his heels. "Lady, you scared the hell out of me. Do you realize you've been unconscious for hours? I was afraid you might have a concussion, or worse."

Chloe pushed her hair from her eyes, grimacing when she felt the strands stiff and uncooperative. She blinked several times against the bright light that caused her eyes to tear. It took her another moment to realize her surroundings weren't what she expected them to be.

Instead of lying on a chaise on the sun deck or even the bed, she was lying on a gritty surface. Instead of a very faint rocking motion, there was none. And instead of the clean white lines of the yacht around her, there were palm trees, other kinds of vegetation and . . . and the ocean wasn't all around her.

She suddenly sat up and wished she hadn't done it as her stomach roiled in protest. She quickly turned her head to one side. If Dalton hadn't held on to her, she probably would have fallen on her face.

"It's okay," he soothed. "I probably didn't get all the water out of you." He wiped her face with his hand. "Here. Just take a sip." He nudged a bottle under her lips.

Chloe grimaced at the tepid water, but was grateful for something to wash her mouth out even as her stomach rebelled.

"What happened?" she asked, handing him back the bottle. "Not to mention where are we and how did we get here?"

"What do you remember?"

She screwed up her face, forgetting her grandmother's rule of moving the facial muscles as little as possible for fear of causing wrinkles.

"It was nighttime. We had a fight." Regret briefly flashed across her face. "And we were on the deck."

"You'd turned ballistic. I never saw you so worked up before. It was an experience." He grinned, but it quickly disappeared.

"I pushed you away and slipped overboard." She looked around, taking stock of her surroundings. "Where is the yacht?"

Gritting her teeth and fighting the dizziness and nausea still rolling around in her stomach, she stood.

When he reached out to help, she slapped his hand away. *"Where the hell are we?"*

"All that mattered was that I get to you. I was afraid you might have hit your head. As it was you were unconscious when I reached you," he said quickly, fearing she would just lose her temper but good. "I called out for help before I jumped into the water, but I don't think anyone heard me. Luckily, I was able to release one of the life rafts before I dove in after you."

"That's not telling me where we are." She touched her clothing, which was equally stiff from dried salt water.

"I don't know."

Chloe exhaled a deep breath. This was one time she wished Dalton would have lied to her.

He remained kneeling on the sand. "I dragged you into the raft, but by then the yacht was too far away. There's a small engine on the raft, but no one bothered to fill it with gas. We were lucky the tide brought us here. I wouldn't worry. I'm sure by now Nando realizes we're not on board and already has search parties out looking for us."

She turned around. All she could see was white sand, blue ocean and palm trees. If the view had been on a picture postcard she would have been impressed. If there was a hotel in the background she would have enjoyed the scenery. Except this wasn't a postcard and there was no hotel as part of the idyllic setting.

She looked down at her arms, the skin already stained a bright pink and feeling prickly from the sun and the sea salt residue.

"Is there any sunscreen in that raft?" she demanded.

He shook his head. "Nothing but your standard rations and some small pieces of equipment. I tried to activate the homing beacon, but it must have gotten wet. I'm sure they're looking for us by now, Chloe."

She was too lost in panic to hear anything he said. "I have no sunscreen. I can't stay out in the sun. It's bad for my skin. And how am I supposed to get this salt out of my hair?" A wild look flashed in her eyes. "It's got to be ruining my hair. And my clothes." She looked down at herself. "They're disgusting!" She suddenly choked up. Her chest heaved with labored breaths. "I can't breathe! I can't breathe!" She wheezed, wrapping her hands around her throat.

Dalton was on his feet in seconds. He ran over to her and grabbed her by her shoulders.

"Cup your hands," he ordered. "Breathe into them. You're hyperventilating. Dammit, Chloe, do as I tell you!" He pulled her hands to her mouth. "Breathe into them! Do it!"

It took several minutes before she felt in control again.

"We can't stay here," she said once she regained her composure.

"Where do you think we can go?"

"We can go back out there." She pointed to sea. "They're not going to look for us here if they think we're still on the water."

"Take a look at the tide," he advised. "It's coming in and pretty strong at that. There's no way we could fight the incoming tide to get the raft out."

"And when it's going out? When will that happen?"

He patted down his hips in an exaggerated gesture. "Damn, I seem to have left my almanac in my other pocket. How the hell would I know when it goes back out? I never had any reason to study the tides!"

"You should be prepared for anything that could come up!" she yelled back. She stepped forward, looking at him as if she was going to grab him by the shirtfront. There was only one problem. He wasn't wearing a shirt. She stared at him, finally seeing for the first time his dark hair lying tangled around his face and cotton pants creased and stiff. A large rip in the fabric revealed a tanned thigh. "We can't just stay here and do nothing!"

"What exactly do you expect us to do, Ms. CEO? Go ahead. Look around and tell me," he shouted, holding his arms out from his sides. "Give me a hint. Pardon me all to hell, but I'm only a dumb artist. I'm not someone with two business degrees who makes million-dollar decisions every five minutes. Come on, make a decision here. *What the hell should we do?*"

Chloe's fury disappeared as rapidly as it erupted. She didn't have to look around to see this was one time she was completely out of her element.

Dalton was right. In the world of business she was a force to be reckoned with.

Here, she was on an island in the middle of the Pacific Ocean. They had a raft with a useless engine; the tide was still incoming so they couldn't even push the raft into the open water if they wanted to. They had no food, very little fresh water and she could feel she was well on her way to suffering a major sunburn. She licked her lips, wincing when she discovered them cracked and chapped. No lip moisturizer, either.

It was taking every ounce of self-control in her body not to break down in tears.

Except her legs were refusing to hold her upright. She fell to the sand like a limp rag doll. The idea of curling up into a tight fetal ball and closing out the world sounded very appealing right about then.

"Chloe?" He dropped down beside her and gathered her onto his lap. "Sweetheart, please don't cry."

She refused to look at him. "I'm not crying."

"No—" the smile in his voice was apparent "—but you want to. Trouble is, your stiff-necked pride won't let you break now." His fingers pressed down on the pressure points along the back of her neck, massaging the tension from her back. "There's times when you don't have to worry about being an adult. When you can just let go. This is one of those times."

"I shouldn't have pushed you," she muttered, letting go when she buried her head against his shoulder. Even with the tang of salt on his skin she imagined she could detect a faint honey almond scent. "If I hadn't been so mad, I wouldn't have pushed you, fallen overboard and forced you to come in after me. Then we wouldn't be on this horrible island."

"We won't be here long," he assured her. "Before you know it, Nando will show up. The resort wasn't all that far from where we were last night, so they shouldn't have any problem in finding us."

"Do you have any idea how far we drifted last night before we ended up here?" she asked, snuggling in closer.

"No." He tucked a stray lock of hair behind her ear. "I wasn't wearing my watch, so I couldn't even tell you what time you fell overboard. And can only estimate the time now."

Her shoulders rose and fell in a huge sigh. "I didn't look at the clock when you came in."

"I'd spent the rest of the evening talking to Leo."

She frowned at the unfamiliar name. "Who?"

"Our esteemed chef. Leonardo. He's a bit crazy, fanatical about his kitchen and funny as hell. We drank wine and talked about life. He had some pretty good stories to relate."

Something else she had forgotten about him. Dalton had the capability to move comfortably among all walks of life. The faint gurgling sound coming from her stomach brought her back to reality.

"Please tell me the raft has something that resembles food?"

He released her and stood, holding out his hand to her. "No problem there. You're probably cranky because you slept through breakfast," he teased.

Dalton led her up the beach until they reached some shade and sat her down. He reached behind several rocks where he had secreted the waterproof canvas bag that held the rations.

"Ah, madam, for today's appetizers we have crackers of the highest grade." He opened a can and drew several out. "I'm afraid the wine's vintage is not one of our best." He handed her one of the water bottles. "To be on the safe side, I suggest we be sparse with the drinking water."

Chloe's appetite disappeared as she realized his words meant there was a chance they might not be found by the end of the day. She started to put her cracker down, but Dalton pushed her hand back up to her mouth.

"You're going to need something in your stomach, so you won't get sick," he advised her.

Dalton watched Chloe closely to make sure she ate. He hurt for her. For once, she was completely out of her element and he wasn't sure what her reaction would be once she recovered from her initial shock. She was still refusing to believe the worst.

He didn't want to tell her everything. He had no idea in what direction they drifted after he'd pulled her into the raft. All he remembered was looking up and watching the yacht glide through the water at an alarming rate. He remembered Leo mentioning they would arrive at the resort today.

He had to hazard a guess the hotel couldn't be all that far away. That it must be situated on a nearby island. He had been relieved to find matches in a waterproof tin. He'd wait until dark before he started up a signal fire. He'd also do a little reconnoitering after he assured himself Chloe would be all right by herself. He hadn't left her side since they washed up on the beach.

He recalled the fear of losing her leaving a sharp coppery taste in his mouth as he urged, then begged, her to open her eyes. He had been ready to scream to the heavens for intervention when she looked up at him with deep violet eyes shadowed with pain.

He had never been so relieved as when she began screaming at him like a banshee with eyes snapping fire and cheeks flushed with hectic color. That was the Chloe he enjoyed seeing. And the one he'd need in case they were marooned here for more than twenty-four hours.

"I'm going to look around," he told her, touching her shoulder with only his fingertips.

Her head snapped up. "What do you mean you're going to look around? You're not leaving me here alone!"

"There's nothing here to harm you. I just want to have a look around."

"How do you know there's nothing dangerous back there?" She looked over her shoulder as if she feared a wild beast would leap onto them at any moment. "This island could be filled with horrible living creatures for all we know."

"I'd give a pretty good guess that the only living creatures on this island are us." He stood. "Don't worry. Just stay close to the beach and you won't have anything to worry about. If you see a ship out there, just run out to the water's edge, jump up and down and wave your arms. They should be able to see you. I won't be long."

Chloe held on to his hands. "I won't let you go."

"Chloe, I just want to have a look around. Nothing more." He vainly tried to release his hands, but she merely tightened her grip. "Chloe, you're breaking my fingers."

She looked up, intent on using all her wiles to keep him by her side. Her eyes first shimmered with unshed tears. Then her lower lip began to tremble.

Dalton squatted down. "Hey, I told you. Don't worry about me. I'll be back in no time. I promise." He rubbed the back of his knuckles against her cheek. "Just yell out if you see anything. I'll come running."

"Promise?"

He smiled and nodded.

Feeling like a lost child, Chloe watched him disappear among the trees and lush vegetation.

She drew her legs up, wrapping her arms around them and rocking back and forth. She had no idea how long she sat there just watching the rolling waves.

"I have no sunscreen, no lip or skin moisturizer." She felt her cheek and bit back a horrified groan at the dryness of her skin. "I'll be a prune by tomorrow." When she lifted her hands to her head and felt the stiff tangled mass she used to call hair she seriously thought about engaging in primal scream therapy.

"No wonder Liza refuses to travel by sea. She's worried about getting shipwrecked."

BY THE TIME Dalton returned, Chloe's imagination had conjured up bloodthirsty scenarios beginning with colorful thoughts of his being captured by cannibals and served up as dinner and ending with his being mauled by a legendary man-eating tiger that no human had seen in more than fifty years.

In an effort to work off her agitation, she paced back and forth along the water's edge, looking out at the open sea as if she could conjure up a rescue ship with her mind. All it accomplished was her reflection on the movie *Jaws* and wondering how close to the beach a great white shark could go.

"Did you find anything?" She ran up to him the moment he appeared.

He shook his head. "Although I did find a treat for milady." He held up two coconuts. "Didn't have to climb up the tree for them, either. Luckily, some have fallen on the ground."

She eyed the dark brown spheres as if they were going to turn into something disgusting at any moment.

"Wonderful. Do you have any idea how we're supposed to open these? I don't know about you, but I usually see coconut in plastic bags at the grocery store."

Dalton shook his head. "I had no idea you even knew what a grocery store was. Come on, Chloe, don't make this rougher than it already is." He used two rocks to crack the shells open. He handed one half to her.

Chloe never knew coconut milk could taste so sweet or quench her thirst. Or that the meat held so much flavor as she daintily dug it out with her fingers. She had no idea her hunger might have had something to do with it.

Finished with her meal, she sat back against a rock with her knees drawn up in front of her as if they were the only protection she had against what was going on around her. She looked up at the sky. Now that her hunger had been sated a little, other thoughts began to form as she realized the sun was starting to set and she couldn't see even a rowboat on the horizon. She didn't feel as hopeful anymore.

"We're not going to be found today, are we?"

Dalton looked up, gauged the time and carefully placed his shell to one side.

"Probably not."

"What will we do?"

He shrugged. "There's plenty of loose fronds around so we should think about building a shelter. It will come in handy if it rains during the night. At least we have fresh water and food. We'll be all right."

Chloe studied her surroundings. Dalton watched her, seeing the frightened expression on her face. He thought of the times he'd seen her happy, in passion and angry, but he couldn't remember ever seeing her afraid.

He sensed she wouldn't believe his assurances that everything would be all right. Right now, he wasn't sure how long they would be here.

He had been too busy concentrating on her while they floated in the raft that he hadn't bothered to notice what direction they traveled in. He noticed a cluster of islands, but he knew distance could be deceiving and had no idea if the resort could be there.

"I didn't see any animals," he said quietly, easily reading what was going through her mind. "I'd say we're the only ones on the island."

She turned back, her eyes wide with fear she didn't seem able to repress. "But you didn't explore the whole island, did you? Or does it look to be nothing more than a sandy strip?"

He shook his head. "I didn't go very far back. I checked more or less along the length of this section. If necessary, I'll explore further tomorrow."

Desperation flared in her eyes. "But we'll be picked up tomorrow. Nando said something about arriving at the resort today, so we can't be all that far from it." She stood and dusted the sand from her pajama bottoms. "You said something about building a shelter. I guess we may as well get to it."

He smiled. This was the take-charge Chloe he needed right now. He stood and gestured for her to precede him.

Under Dalton's direction, Chloe helped drag palm fronds out to the edge of the beach where several boulders would provide a suitable shelter.

She labored without complaint even as the fronds cut into her hands and a once-immaculate manicure was ruined. When they finished, Chloe's body gleamed with sweat and her breathing was raspy. She collapsed against a rock.

"Aerobics doesn't prepare a person for this," she said. She glared at him. "You're hardly even breathing hard."

She did notice that while he wasn't as out of breath as she was, his bare chest was also covered with sweat and his cotton pants clung to his lower hips. He had grown frustrated with the torn fabric and used the knife to cut it away, so he now wore abbreviated shorts that bared tanned legs dusted with fine dark hair. His jaw was covered with dark stubble that added to his pirate demeanor. She decided all he needed was a gold earring to complete the picture.

"Clean living." He pulled the canvas bag and a tarp from the raft into the shelter. He laid the tarp on the ground and brushed the sand from it.

"Where did you learn about all this?"

"You experience all sorts of survival techniques in the navy." He upended the contents of the bag onto the tarp and sorted them out. "Crackers, some freeze-dried jerky, a knife, small first-aid kit." He suddenly chuckled. "Damn. No pâté or caviar. You'd think Bella Skin would have provided better rations on their life rafts." He gestured for her to sit in front of him. He opened the first-aid kit. "Give me your hands." He opened the tube of antiseptic cream and carefully dabbed it on the scratches. "We can't afford for these to get infected."

Chloe winced as the cream melted into the scratches and abraded skin.

"I guess there isn't any hand cream in there, either," she commented with false lightheartedness.

He smiled. "Sorry. Maybe we should make a list of what would be suitable items for their passengers who happen to get shipwrecked."

"French mineral water?" she suggested. "Maybe even champagne for those beach suppers."

"Steaks."

"Chocolate."

"A tiny stereo."

She looked glassy eyed. "Cigarettes."

He peered at her closely. "You don't smoke. And you don't eat chocolate."

"If you had examined my makeup bag a little more you would have found the chocolate stashed in a false bottom along with a pack of cigarettes and a lighter," she confessed.

"A false bottom?"

She nodded. "I use it when I take trips with Amanda."

Dalton shook his head, amused by her admission. "I can't believe it. The lady has vices. Dangerous ones, too. Isn't Dame Amanda known for saying smoking damages the skin and chocolates further ruin it? What would she do if she knew her favorite, and only, granddaughter indulges in both?"

"She'd have me taken away to a secret location where I could be deprogrammed until I vowed to give up both." Chloe carefully rubbed her palms together so the cream would be better dispersed. "Liza buys them for me."

He shook his head. "That is really sick, Chloe. Is it really worth it?"

"The chocolate is." Her eyes gleamed as she thought of her favorite treat. She immediately wished she hadn't dreamed about it since she couldn't indulge herself.

"Why would you work for a woman who unnerves you so much? With your skills you could go to any company you wanted to."

"I don't work for Amanda. She retired and I'm in charge now. Besides, it's a family company and needs to be run by family."

Dalton was silent for a moment. "Who thought of this merger?"

"I did."

"Were you able to work this idea up by yourself?"

"Of course not! The board had to approve it."

"And who's the leading force behind the board."

"Aman—" She took a deep breath. "My grandmother started Chrysalis at a time when women weren't in the work force. If she still offers opinions, it's because she was the one who began it and she wants to keep the enthusiasm she's always generated there. If she hadn't given me the backing she had when she retired I would have had more trouble with the other executives. A lot of people there felt they should have taken over instead of me, even if it was always known only a Sumner would be in charge. I think some of them had the hope of succeeding Amanda since my mother preferred to remain in charge of the lab. Instead, Amanda waited until she felt I was ready to take over."

Dalton changed his position until he sat cross-legged. He looked down at his lap where his hands rested on his knees.

"From the time you began working there you knew you would take over," he murmured. "In the beginning, you treated it like a joke. You talked about outlandish colors like purple blush and blue lipstick." A faint smile touched his lips. "I always liked the idea of the eye shadow colors you wanted named after fruits. Especially the one called Guava."

"You remember that?" she whispered.

He nodded. "I remember a lot from those days when you insisted the eye shadows needed to be more bright and colorful. That was when you still considered it fun instead of work."

If she had any idea a faint line creased her brow while he spoke she would have instantly relaxed her face. That her agitation overrode all caution was obvious.

"Running a company isn't a game, Dalton. It's a great deal of hard work."

He smiled at her huffy tone. "Now that's Amanda talking."

She puffed up at what she thought was his condescending tone. "No, it's *me* talking."

He shook his head. "You only say that because Amanda taught you so well. There's more to life than the company, Chloe. You used to believe it. You need to rediscover that."

"I have a very rich life," she hotly argued.

"When was the last time you took a trip just for fun?"

"I was in Italy just nine months ago."

"For fun or to scope out Bella Skin?"

She reddened at his direct hit, then quickly rallied. "You were in Europe to work with other sculptors. That doesn't sound like a trip purely for fun."

"I also took time off to go explore the countryside. I went out and talked to people, relaxed at sidewalk cafés, visited museums and not just to study other people's work, either," he quickly mentioned. "You know, maybe this is just what you need."

Chloe looked at him warily. "What do you mean by that?"

"Maybe this is fate's way of telling you it's time to slow down and reflect on what you really want from life." He dropped back on the tarp cushioning his head with his hands.

She jumped to her feet and almost lost her balance as the sand shifted under her swift movements. She waved her arms to keep herself upright.

"Are you nuts? What do you think you're say- ing?"

He winced at her shriek. "Could you speak a little louder, please? I don't think the residents in New Zealand heard you."

Chloe began pacing back and forth.

"Slow down? Reflect on my life? It's just fine, thank you very much! I'm not the one who probably lives in some broken-down garret with antiquated plumbing and has to work as a *husband,*" she railed at him. "You don't even have a car!"

"How do you know that?" he countered.

She wasn't stopping now. "Easy! You say a car owns you instead of you owning it. You probably don't have one due to some misguided principle!"

Dalton crossed his legs at the ankle and made him- self comfortable as he listened to Chloe rant and rave as she paced back and forth in front of the shelter. He didn't bother to correct her erroneous statement about a car. Although, there were still days he felt as if his vintage Austin Martin did indeed own him.

He calculated that her tirade should keep her occupied for about an hour. By the time she ran out of steam, she'd be feeling tired enough to listen to reason. And hopefully not try to kill him when she discovered they'd be sharing the shelter.

Chapter Nine

"You intend for us to what?"

Dalton winced as Chloe's shrill voice assaulted his ears.

He turned out to be wrong. It had taken her a good forty-five minutes over his estimation before she finally wound down from her tantrum. He had expected a reaction to his announcement. Just not such a loud and vocal one when he casually told her about their sleeping arrangements.

"It isn't all that different than when we were on board the *Bella.*"

She glared at him as she stood there with her fists braced on her hips.

"There was a very good reason for our doing it there. That doesn't mean we have to here."

"Sweetheart, maybe your memory is better than mine, but I don't remember our actually ever doing *it.*"

Her jaw worked furiously. Her fingers curved as if they wanted nothing more than to fasten themselves around his throat.

"Don't be smart. You know very well what I mean."

He was impressed with her self-control. He honestly thought she would have attacked him by now.

Chloe's threatening gaze should have seared him to the bone. She spun on her heel, almost lost her balance in the shifting sand and stalked down to the water's edge.

Dalton frowned. "Where are you going?" he called after her.

"For a swim," she yelled over her shoulder.

"Aren't you afraid of sharks?" He couldn't resist baiting her.

"Considering everything else you've called me, I would think there would be no problem of the sharks welcoming me as one of their own." She waded into the water and struck out with strong strokes.

Once assured she wasn't in any trouble, Dalton set about to build a small fire. He squatted down on his heels.

"If the sharks are smart, they'll stay out of her way."

"YOU'RE ENJOYING THIS, aren't you?"

"Enjoying what?" Dalton had examined the knife, found it a little too dull for his taste and was busy sharpening it on a stone.

"All this." She waved her hands around. "I was thrown overboard. You dove over and we both ended up in a raft that beached us on an island in the middle of the Pacific Ocean. We could die here and you're acting as if you're a reincarnation of Tarzan. Dammit, you're having fun!" she accused as if he had deliberately planned their disaster.

"I haven't begun swinging on vines. The ones I've seen haven't looked all that sturdy." He scraped the blade against his thumb to check its edge. Satisfied it was sharp enough he put the stone to one side.

Chloe twisted from a cross-legged position to kneeling.

Dalton looked up. "Are we bored?"

"I'm not used to doing nothing. Nor am I used to sitting in sand that makes my skin itch. I'm positive there's some kind of tiny bug that's biting me all over! I can feel the sun and salt air drying out my skin and turning it into a wrinkled mass. All I can do is watch the waves roll out," she said darkly, looking down at her hands. "Louise is going to have a fit when she sees my nails."

Dalton's gaze followed hers. Barely twelve hours and her hands were already red and chapped with several broken nails and chipped polish.

"I'd say this time she'll have a major breakdown. Make sure to give her a big tip. Hey." He reached across and took one of her hands in his. "It's not so bad. We're not in the raft, it's not raining, there's no sign of snow and you're not stuck with someone who doesn't know how to build a shelter."

Her smile was brief and unwilling. "You're not going to let me sit here and feel sorry for myself, are you?"

He brought the sadly abused hand to his lips. "No, I'm not."

Chloe suddenly moved over to him and snuggled in his lap. With his arms wrapped around her, she finally felt comfortable. And safe.

As if sensing she needed comforting more than loving, Dalton indulged himself with only a light kiss on her forehead.

"It's a perfect night for ghost stories," he said absently.

She shuddered. "No way! I don't want to hear those gory tales you used to tell. There were nights I was convinced a hideous monster was going to break into the apartment and turn us into pâté."

Dalton rubbed his cheek against the top of her head. He could hear the faint rasp of stubble against her hair. "You loved it and you know it. Did I ever tell you about a sixty-foot stingray that could crawl on land after dark?"

"No! Not that!"

As he heard her protest end in laughter, Dalton knew Chloe would be all right. At least, she'd be fine until morning came and she realized they were still there and not about to leave in the near future.

"I CAN'T HANDLE this!"

Dalton looked up from the fire he had been feeding green wood so it would send up black smoke, in hopes the fire would be seen by anything resembling a search party.

He had been right. Everything changed from the moment Chloe had woken up that morning all warm and soft in his arms. After that, she turned into a perfect Shakespearean shrew bent on making life hell for both of them.

She first organized their breakfast with the aplomb of a five-star general. Then she insisted he build a signal fire on the beach. After that, she suggested they search out the nearby trees to see if they could find any more fallen coconuts. Once they'd found a small supply of them, she took off for a wash in the ocean while he fought the incoming tide as he swam out. The battle with the ocean was one he didn't mind losing. In his mind, it was easier to fight nature than to fight Chloe.

"Now what?"

She held out a hank of hair. "It's a mess. I can't do anything with it. It's tangled so badly I can't even braid it. It feels like rope! A horrible, disgusting, dirty rope!"

Dalton looked at the raven curls made even wilder from her swim and the morning breeze.

"I am so sorry. I'm afraid the manufacturers of the survival kit didn't think to provide a comb or shampoo and hair conditioner for milady," he said sarcastically.

"The hell with shampoo and conditioner! I want to cut it all off."

Dalton thought he had heard everything, but this was a new one for him.

"Why don't you wait and see," he suggested. "If you cut all your hair off and a search party shows up, you're going to be really upset with yourself."

"If I have to deal with this much longer, I swear I'm going to tear it out by the roots." She stared at his hair, which didn't appear to look as bad as hers although the usual slight waves had been subdued from a recent swim.

While his hair was still wet he'd settled for slicking it back and using a strip of the material he'd cut off his pants yesterday to keep it pulled back in a halfway neat ponytail.

He crooked his finger in a "come here" gesture. Chloe walked slowly toward him. He gestured for her to turn around.

"Chloe, did you ever read *Lord of the Flies?*"

She instantly spun around. "That is *not* funny!"

He spun her around so her back was to him, and she couldn't see the grin stretching his lips.

"Sorry, I couldn't help it. Now let's see about this so-called disaster you call hair," he told her, combing her locks back from her temples with his fingers. He rummaged around in the pack and pulled out another strip of fabric that he used to tie her hair back. "There, that should help." He ran his hands down her arms. "Tell you what. Why don't we do some exploring?"

She gazed toward the fire, then the horizon, as if a ship would suddenly appear.

"What if someone flies overhead or a ship comes by? Won't the fire have to be kept going? We'll have to be here to see them and so they'll see us."

"I'll put enough wood on it to keep it going for a while. If they see the smoke, they'll come ashore to investigate. They'll see the packs and I'm sure will wait for us," he told her. "Come on, it will be good for you to take a walk. The exercise will help clear your head." He took hold of her hand. "Maybe we'll find a temple built by some ancient Polynesian race that's no longer in existence."

Against her better judgment, she allowed him to pull her up the beach.

"Terrific, and maybe by walking on ancient ground we'll unleash a curse where the dead will come back to life and demand a sacrifice. Us."

He shook his head. "And you talk about my vivid imagination."

As they walked through the thick vegetation, Chloe was aware of the temperature rising. While it had been hot on the beach, it was much warmer here. She was surprised by the humming sound that seemed to echo all around her.

She tugged on Dalton's arm. Her fingers tightened as they dug into his skin.

"What's that noise?" she demanded.

He frowned. "What noise?"

"The clicking, the humming and whatever else it is. What is it?"

He stopped and listened for a moment. "Insects."

"Bugs!" She could have said monsters in the same tone of voice.

"Yeah. They're nothing to worry about as long as you don't bother them."

"What about snakes?" she asked in a barely audible voice.

"Last I heard, Hawaii doesn't have snakes, so I doubt the other islands have any," he said.

"That's a consolation."

Dalton stopped and turned his head in two directions. "Do you hear it?"

She edged closer to him. "Hear what?"

He grabbed her hand and pulled her alongside him as he quickened his steps.

"Let's just hope it's what I think it is."

"Hey, slow down! You've got longer legs than I do," she protested, almost tripping over a fallen branch he easily stepped over.

Any other argument Chloe could have come up with was abruptly silenced as they made their way through the trees where they found a tiny clearing festooned with brightly colored flowers releasing a fragrance that Chloe immediately wanted bottled. But it was the small rocky incline with water spilling over it and into a natural pool that captured her attention.

"Oh," she murmured, dropping to her knees. She cupped her hands in the water, then paused. "It's okay, isn't it?"

Dalton dropped beside her and dipped several fingers in the water, then touched the tips to his tongue.

"It's fresh," he announced with a smile.

Chloe didn't have to think twice. She immediately ran over and threw herself into the water. She squealed happily as she bobbed up.

"It's great!"

Dalton didn't need a second invitation. He dove in and came up close to her.

"At least we can wash the salt off our skin," Chloe happily told him. "I was beginning to itch so badly from the dryness."

"Poor baby," he mocked.

"Poor baby?" She covered his head with her hands and pushed him under the water. Then shrieked when he pulled her under with him.

Chloe was released the moment they came up for air. She kicked herself onto her back and floated around the perimeter of the pool.

"However did you miss this yesterday?" she asked.

"I had traveled in the other direction then. You know, I think those are mangoes up there." He pointed toward one of the nearby trees. "We should take some back with us."

"All we need to make it perfect is music in the background and slaves to bring us champagne and chocolate," Chloe said from her prone position in the water.

"There's that mention of chocolate again," Dalton teased.

"For now, I'll settle for fresh water and the promise of no snakes." She laughed, wiggling her toes. "But once I'm back among civilization, I am going to consume a five-pound box all by myself. Then I'm going to smoke an entire pack of cigarettes."

"Yeah, and afterward you'll be so sick you won't want either ever again."

"That's what you think."

Weary from her swim, Chloe swam over to the pond edge and collapsed on the ground.

"How could there be fresh water here?" she asked him.

Dalton followed her and dropped down beside her. "Who knows? But think of the number of people who probably once populated all of these outer islands. They had to have drinking water." He picked up several flower vines and idly worked them into a braid.

Chloe rolled over onto her side.

"Dalton, if I ask you a question will you tell me the truth?"

He looked at her with eyes filled with amusement. "Have you ever known me to lie?"

She smiled. "No, but there's always the first time."

"Then ask away."

"Have you known any success with your work?"

"I haven't become famous or rich, but my work has its merits." He suddenly grinned. "Maybe I should have taken a commission from Lucretia. Although, I think that kind of work would only have made me infamous."

"What kind of artwork did she want?"

Dalton leaned over and whispered in her ear. Chloe's eyes widened into amethyst saucers.

"She really wanted those in her garden? Did you ever see it?"

He solemnly nodded.

"And that's what she had erected there for everyone to see?"

He nodded again. His lips twitched with mirth.

Chloe considered the description.

"That is very...interesting," she said for lack of a better description.

"You had to see it to believe it." He idly twined a damp lock of her hair around his finger. "It seems the fresh water softened your hair. Aren't you glad you didn't cut it?"

She could sense his body heat reaching out to her. Enveloping her. For a brief second, her eyes dropped, noting the way the damp fabric of his pants molded to his hips. She was surprised to see he was aroused.

"It's something that just seems to happen when I'm around you," he said without apology.

Chloe's nipples tightened in reaction. Dalton's gaze lowered, noting the way the front of her top dipped and molded to the peaks.

"Dalton." Her eyes shone like luminous jewels.

He turned his head and looked at her, waiting for what she wanted to say.

She took a deep breath, looking as if she was gathering her courage.

"That night?" She took another deep breath. "I wished you'd taken me instead of a cold shower."

That was all she said. It was enough.

He gently drew her against the length of his body and rolled over onto his back. Chloe's mouth fastened on his in a light, teasing kiss. She giggled at his growl of frustration and proceeded to drop more kisses around the edge of his mouth, giggling at the feel of his beard against her tender skin.

"Yes," he muttered, wrapping his hands around her head. He brought her face back to his for a deep kiss meant to satisfy them both. His tongue thrust between her lips, possessing her the same way his body intended to.

Chloe flowed against him, feeling the heat of his body envelope her as he curved his legs around hers, angling her into the aroused cradle of his thighs.

"Do you realize how long I've dreamed about this?" he muttered, not caring if she answered him. He knew he had to verbalize the way he felt. Tell her what had been going on inside of him for so long. "There we were, on the *Bella* together, posing as the husband and wife we used to be. But I still can't touch you the way I want to or kiss you the way I want to."

"Until now," she whispered.

He nodded. "Until now."

"Then I suggest you get to it." She punctuated each word with a kiss and saucy flick of the tongue.

Dalton didn't hesitate.

This time he crushed her mouth under his, taking what she so willingly offered. He delved and plundered her mouth like the pirate she visualized him as.

This time there would be no going back for them. No untimely interruptions.

Chloe placed her palms against his chest, feeling the light dusting of hair prickle her skin. She rubbed her nose against the hard surface, laughing softly as the hair tickled her face.

Dalton slid his hand under her top, feeling the warmth of her breast, the aroused peak of her nipple, against his palm.

"Chloe!" he groaned against her parted lips. "Before we go any further, I need to show some responsibility, although any kind of sanity is pretty much past me. Honey, I'm afraid I left my wallet back on board."

It took a moment for her to understand his cryptic words. It wasn't easy to think when he was circling the perimeter of her breasts with his fingertips, arousing her even more since he never fully covered the aching mounds.

"It's safe." She stumbled over the words. Her head was whirling. At that moment, the last thing she wanted to do was count days!

Dalton wasted no time in pulling her tank top over her head and working the bottoms down her hips and legs. He hissed a sharp breath between his teeth as he gazed down at the pearly white skin.

"How did I ever get to be so lucky as to have you in my life?" he muttered, almost tearing off his shorts.

Chloe smiled and opened her arms. "Pure luck."

Dalton rolled over onto his back. He pulled her on top, laughing at the startled expression on her face that quickly smoothed out into a beatific smile.

"I didn't think you'd appreciate having that lovely behind bruised by the ground," he told her, resting his arousal against the moist delta between her thighs. He made no movement to enter her. He gritted his teeth against the compulsion to make love to her. He wanted to feel her surround him again. To experience the pulsing rhythm they always shared. He eased his way inside, feeling the tight heat wrap itself around him like a sensual glove. Chloe's eyes glowed with deep purple fires as she stared down into his face.

Dalton was determined to take this slow and easy, even if it killed him. He picked up her hand, placing her fingers at his lips. He moistened them with his tongue. Laved them gently as he looked up at her with simmering dark eyes. Then he wrapped his lips around each finger, curling his tongue around them. Chloe's features tightened.

Each time she tried to shift her hips in an effort to arouse him into moving, he merely stilled her movements with a firm grip on her hips.

"No," he whispered.

"Yes," she whispered back, leaning down to brush her lips against his. "It's paradise. Anything goes."

"How right you are, but let's try it this way." He barely flexed his hips.

Except Chloe was impatient. She felt a burning sensation settle deep within her soul at his possession. But she wanted more. She wanted to feel the fire she sensed burning inside him. The storm that used to rock them both as they enjoyed each other. Instead, he seemed to want it to last forever. There was only one problem with that. She wasn't sure she could last.

Chloe tightened her inner muscles and smiled as Dalton's nostrils flared in reaction.

"You're playing with fire, lady," he warned in a husky voice.

She leaned over, deliberately brushing her breasts against his chest as her hand roamed southward. "Then why don't you do something about it?"

He grasped her hips again, preventing any movement on her part, then thrust upward in barely perceptible movements that sent off small explosions within them both.

Chloe gasped as she imagined she could feel him in every part of her being.

"Dalton," she keened, straining to move, but he still prevented her.

"This is all for you," he told her just as she exploded into tiny fragments.

"THAT WAS INCREDIBLE." Chloe rolled over onto her side so she could stare at his profile.

"Thank you. I thought I was pretty good."

She playfully struck him. "Don't smirk! Why can't you be humble for once?"

"Probably because humility isn't a part of me."

Chloe's gaze moved over Dalton's body. Tanned, lean with the long muscles of a man who honed his body to razor sharpness. She wanted him again. She lowered her lashes to keep her hunger a secret. For the time being.

She settled for tangling her fingers in the light dusting of hair on his chest. She remembered the first time she had touched him like this. How she thought of his skin so hot and silky under her fingertips. And how she enjoyed watching the pleasure suffuse his features as she explored him. It had been Dalton's complete self-confidence that encouraged her to find her own self-awareness. One she hadn't been able to feel since their divorce.

She draped her leg over his thigh, comfortable with their nudity. She could almost delude herself into thinking this was all a dream and she would wake up on the yacht. Still, could her imagination be this creative?

"If nothing else, there were never complaints about our sex life," she murmured.

He rolled over onto his side. "Then what were the complaints?"

She took a deep breath. "Truth?"

He shot her a wry smile. "Even if it hurts."

Chloe sat up and reached for her clothing. She didn't speak until her top and pants were on, as if she needed that tiny protection.

"I was brought up to believe that the business was everything. It was brought to home that the Sumner women couldn't have a long-term relationship because it wasn't within us. Wasn't in our genes," she began. "Men had trouble understanding just how important the company was and that they would have to take a back seat to it. The resentment always ruined things."

"In other words, you couldn't find it within yourselves to share?"

She ignored his sarcasm.

"It was the men who couldn't share us with the business. My grandfather hated the idea of my grandmother becoming a success when his own venture failed. My father loved my mother, but couldn't stand Amanda. He thought he could walk right into the executive suite and resented the fact he'd have to earn the right. So he went to work for the competition and refused to acknowledge me as his daughter."

"That could have been proved in court," he mentioned, silently furious with the man for not acknowledging a woman who was so special. And pitied him for missing out on so much.

She shook her head. "Amanda refused to have it dragged through the courts and my mother decided she was better off without him. I think that's why she preferred to remain in R and D. She figured it was safer."

"And then us," Dalton said softly. "You never gave me a chance, did you?"

She felt his emotional withdrawal as strongly as if he physically walked away from her.

"We just couldn't make it work," she began.

He waved his hand in the air, asking for her silence.

"No, you didn't even bother to see if we could make things work. You didn't try. You blithely decided, in your own domineering way, that there was no way in hell we could blend our two lives into something beautiful. It was easier to walk away than make things work." He spoke slowly and deliberately to wound. "I'm not sure if you're just lazy or cowardly."

Chloe's fury had her trembling as she shot to her feet.

"That is a despicable thing to say!"

He jumped to his feet. "Why? Because it's the truth? That's your problem, Chloe. You always refused to face the truth. When things got rough, you preferred to hide your head in the sand and let *Grandma* take care of things for you because it was the easy way out."

Until Dalton, Chloe never knew what a violent thought was. Her hand flashed out to strike, but he was just as quick. His fingers braceleted her wrist.

"Your biggest mistake has always been the way you telegraph your moves," he said softly. "Now I'm going to make a suggestion I think would be advisable for both of us right now. I'm going for a walk. Why don't you take a swim to cool off?"

Chloe's angry response brought a smile to his lips.

"Sorry, baby, but it's not physically possible," he murmured in her ear. "I hate to think what could happen if Dame Amanda heard you now. I bet she'd happily wash your mouth out with soap but good."

He took his time pulling his shorts on and walked away.

Chloe glared at him. She suddenly wished she had a weapon in her hand. The idea of Dalton writhing in pain held distinct possibilities. Instead, she took his suggestion and dove back into the water. Only a good long swim would calm her down right now.

Dalton deliberately walked in a different direction. As he hiked, he thought of his making love to Chloe. The way she felt against him. Only by spitting out a few curses did he finally regain control.

He wasn't sure how long he walked until he realized the vegetation had changed and that the faint sounds in the air didn't seem to come from any birds.

He followed the sounds until he reached a row of palm trees. He peered through the foliage and exhaled a low whistle.

The sight before him was a shock.

Tennis courts, a swimming pool in the distance, a lush green golf course and white buildings in the distance. People sunbathing around the pool, others running back and forth on the tennis courts and several following the little white balls.

Dalton had no doubt that what he was looking at was the Bella Resort in all its splendor. No wonder they hadn't seen a rescue boat yet. He doubted they had thought to check the other side of the island. Although he was sure, in time, they would think of it.

He walked backward until he was sure there wasn't a chance of his being seen.

As he retraced his steps, Dalton wondered how much mayhem Chloe was going to cause when she discovered they weren't all that far from the resort.

He wasn't sure when he made the decision. As he came closer to the other side of the island he knew he wasn't going to tell her about his discovery. Not just yet. Not until he could get things straightened out between them.

"When she finds out I didn't tell her—and I know she will—she'll kill me for sure."

Chapter Ten

Dalton was worried. When he returned to the waterfall and didn't find Chloe he feared that she had wandered off in search of him and got lost...or that she had somehow stumbled onto the resort.

Luckily, sanity took over before he overreacted. If anything, she was back at the camp, he assured himself.

He headed in the direction of the beach, feeling relief flow through his body when he saw the fire still going strong and Chloe standing down at the water's edge.

He smiled at the sight of a ramrod-stiff posture that would make any etiquette instructor proud. No matter what went on in her life, he knew she would meet it with head held high, back straight and war flags flying. That's what he loved about her.

"Have you seen anything out there?"

She turned around. The moment he saw the set chin and lack of emotion in her gaze, he knew the fevered moment at the waterfall was well past. He regretted that because the idea of repeating the scene later on tonight had been forming in the back of his mind. He guessed he'd just have to come up with an alternative.

"Lots of water and what looked like an occasional dolphin," she replied in clipped tones. "What about you? Find anything during your travels?"

"Nothing of importance," he lied without a qualm as he walked down the beach to where she stood. "I said I was willing to hear the truth even if it hurt. I had hoped it would go both ways. Obviously, I was wrong."

If it were possible, her body stiffened even more. If looks could kill he would be a burning corpse on the sand. "You implied I'm a spoiled brat."

"No, I didn't imply that. If I thought that, I would have said so. I only said that if you want to keep something badly enough, you should be willing to fight for it. Since it seems you didn't fight back then, you didn't give a damn about our remaining together."

Pain flashed briefly across her features as his blunt words struck more than a few nerves. She crossed her arms in front of her chest in a classic defensive posture.

"We need to talk about it, Chloe," Dalton said gently, feeling her pain. He knew she would have to feel the agony if they were going to have the chance to go on and heal past wounds. But he wanted more than what they once had. This time, he wanted all of her. "We need to let it all out and see where it will lead us."

She turned away, looking out over the water. "Why? All we do is fight."

"So we fight. Even that's communicating. All we need to do is set up a few ground rules and take it from there."

She didn't turn back around, but he could tell she was thinking over what he said.

"Such as?"

He thought about it for a moment. "No slinging personal insults. No walking away no matter how rough things get. A willingness to take what's dished out. And speaking the truth at all times."

She flinched at the last statement. Now he knew she had lied to him a few times. He only hoped her lies weren't about anything important to the two of them.

"When shall we begin this therapy session?" she asked finally. Obviously, that was her way of agreeing with his terms.

He didn't want to take any chance of her losing her courage. "Now?"

She nodded jerkily. She still hadn't looked at him.

"You always talked about how much you hated my working late at night." Her voice was barely audible over the sound of the waves rolling out to sea. "It was important I work late and you refused to accept it."

"I hated the idea that you could have been attacked coming out of your office. I worried about you every time you were late and didn't call me to let me know."

She turned around and faced him. "Then why didn't you tell me that instead of always complaining about all the hours I worked? You kept telling me I preferred my job to you."

"I couldn't help it if my fears mixed with my words and usually came out wrong," he argued. "Just like the times you complained about all the hours I had to spend in my studio."

"Of course, I did! We'd plan to go out to dinner or have to meet some of my business associates and you'd never show! I couldn't even call you because more often than not the phone's ringer was turned off." She took a deep breath as she plunged on, "And then you'd always refuse to wear a tie! How many restaurant maître d's did you anger because you told them ties were an evil invention!"

"Just because a restaurant serves their meals on fine china and crystal doesn't mean a man has to wear a tie!" he debated. "I always wore a nice suit. What more could they want?"

"They wanted a damn tie!" she screamed, throwing up her arms and waving them around. "And that horrible dust! You were always covered with a white film! Not to mention the cleaners could never get the clay out of your clothing. A couple of laundries I took your clothing to asked me not to come back! Can you imagine how embarrassing that was?"

"Embarrassing to you? What about me? No self-respecting artist has their clothes sent to the laundry." He stared up at the sky. "Tell me, did Michelangelo send his smocks to the laundry? Would Picasso have his clothing dry-cleaned? *No!* I buy us a washer and dryer and you ruin them the first time you use it!"

"You're being sarcastic," she said stiffly. Her cheeks burned a bright red.

"I'm asking questions I want answers to. Sarcasm has nothing to do with it."

"All I ever asked is that you showed up for appointments on time and that you wore a tie."

"What about what *I* asked for? Or doesn't that count?"

"Such as?"

"Such as your willingness to obey your grandmother's dictates without a murmur. I don't think you'd argue with her if your life depended on it."

"Dictates?" she echoed. "What dictates?"

"The time you went with her to Switzerland for six weeks," he reminded her.

She flushed. "That was business."

Dalton's jaw worked furiously. "Business. How many days of that six weeks did you spend on business?" When she didn't answer right away, he pressed, "How many damn days, Chloe?"

"Four," she whispered.

He heaved a sigh of relief as he realized she spoke the truth. "Four days out of six weeks. Six weeks, which comes to forty-two days. Barely one-tenth of the time gone."

"Amanda wasn't feeling well and wanted to visit a health spa nearby since we were in the area."

"Yes, I remember what happened only too well," Dalton said wryly. "The two of you ran into the grandson of one of her old acquaintance's there, didn't you? A clothing manufacturer from London, wasn't he? Just the kind of man she wanted you to know."

"I'm sure I don't remember," Chloe said stiffly, crossing her arms in front of her again.

"I remember enough. We had been married barely a month before she whisked you off to Switzerland for an alleged business trip and didn't waste any time introducing you to her idea of eligible men." This time, the pain was etched on his face. "She hadn't accepted me from the beginning."

"You never gave her a chance!"

"She didn't give me a chance, either!" he shot back.

She rubbed her arms. "She was upset because we eloped instead of our having a conventional wedding."

"You said you didn't want a long engagement," he reminded her. "The truth was, you never told her we were going to get married, did you? Dame Amanda hadn't approved of me from that first time you took me out to her house for Sunday brunch. Once she found out I was recently out of the navy and working in clay, she immediately decided I wasn't good enough for you. She never bothered to find out what kind of man I was. What did she tell you? Not to see me again? Seems the times we were together changed after that. And when I proposed you were all for flying to Vegas to get married. Your mother accepted me, but it seemed as if her opinion didn't mean a damn to you. Only Amanda's did."

"That's not true!" she argued, but the hot blush coloring her face said otherwise.

"Fine, tell me exactly what Dame Amanda said when you told her we were married."

"That was more than six years ago," she said evasively. "I don't remember."

"Considering you have a near photographic memory, I'm sure you can recall every word."

"I told you. I don't remember." Except she couldn't keep her gaze steady. Another sign she was lying.

"What did she say?" he roared, feeling his patience ebb like the tide.

"She said she couldn't have chosen a more unsuitable husband for me if she'd tried!" she screamed back.

Dalton inhaled a deep breath. "Well, we finally got past that hurdle, didn't we?" he said in a calmer voice. "Fine, you said your piece. Now it's my turn. I still want to know why you let Amanda handle the divorce. I want to know why you wouldn't take my calls and why you returned my letters."

She looked at him in disbelief. "I never received any calls or letters from you during our separation."

"I called your office and was told you wouldn't take my calls and I wasn't to bother you again. My letters were returned unopened," he told her.

Chloe couldn't accuse Dalton of lying. And if he did that, she knew who made sure his calls weren't accepted and letters returned. During that time, she had stayed with Amanda, allowing her grandmother to coddle her and take care of the details of the divorce.

"She did what she thought was best," she murmured, feeling an odd ache deep within her heart. If she hadn't retreated into her own shell back then, she might have realized something was wrong and taken her own steps to contact Dalton.

"Best? For whom?" he asked. "To this day, I still don't know why you left me. What did I do wrong, Chloe? Did I ignore you too much? Was it because I missed so many of those dinners? What about the time when you came down with the flu and couldn't even lift your head? I didn't leave the apartment once back then! I was so worried about you, I couldn't sleep! You don't know the fear I felt that you'd get so ill you'd never come back to me." He reached out and grabbed hold of her shoulders. "I know you won't agree with me, but I never considered those dinners urgent. What was important to me was you."

Chloe's lower lip quivered. "Then why didn't you say so?"

He stepped back, stunned by her words. "Why didn't I say so? I told you how much I cared every time

I held you in my arms, kissed you, made love to you. Dammit, Chloe, you were my life!''

She stared at him, stunned by his words.

"But you never came out and said so," she whispered. She blinked against the moisture filling her eyes, then felt the tears trickle down her cheeks. "Why didn't you put it into words? Why didn't you tell me?"

"We were in tune with everything else. How was I supposed to know you didn't realize how I felt?" he told her. "Chloe, please don't cry."

"I can't help it." She sniffed, wiping her nose with the back of her hand. "You're telling me something that's upset my entire life balance. I can't just calmly stand here."

He stepped forward and wiped away her tears with his thumbs.

"I really didn't know you called or wrote," she said between sniffles.

He ran his fingertips across her cheeks, lifting them to his lips and tasting the salty moisture. "I figured that back then."

"Why didn't you come to the office?"

"I did. Security was under orders to escort me out of the building."

Chloe made a face. "Amanda did a number on both of us, didn't she?" An agonizing thought suddenly occurred to her. "She didn't offer you money, did she?"

"No, she had more class than that," he admitted. "I think she also knew I would tell her what she could do with the money."

A glimmer of a smile appeared between the tears. "You really would have told her off?"

"In spades." His brief smile disappeared and an intensity that struck Chloe to the pit of her stomach replaced it. "Darling, no one else mattered to me but you. No one ever did."

"I always thought artists put their work first," she said so softly he almost couldn't hear her.

Amanda again. He silently cursed the older woman for planting those thoughts into Chloe's head. He always thought she had self-confidence, and it was only recently that he came to realize she didn't possess enough to fight her grandmother.

"I should have been more open with you verbally instead of just physically," he said quietly. "Then you wouldn't have ever had any doubts about us."

Chloe lifted her hand in a gesture of frustration. "There had to be more than that back then. We couldn't have split up just because of that." She grimaced. "Or because of Amanda."

"She wanted someone to rule the empire and she didn't want a prince consort cluttering up the background."

Chloe turned away. At that moment she wasn't sure she could look at Dalton and think of the truth smacking her in the face.

"She never truly lied. She never tried to pay you off," she murmured. "She just planted the seeds and let them grow. With the family curse of the Sumner women unable to hold on to a man, it wasn't difficult for me to believe her." She spun around and walked toward Dalton. When she reached him, she threw her arms around his waist and just held on.

He threaded his fingers through her hair, dragging her face up to his. He smiled at the look on her face.

"Are you ready to hear about how I hated your using my toothpaste?"

At that moment, the levity was badly needed.

Chloe's laughter mixed with her tears. "You hated my using your toothpaste?"

He kept on hugging her tightly, unwilling to release her.

"Sure, I did. You always squeezed from the middle instead of the end and you never put the top back on." He made mock face of disgust. "And you always left the bathroom in a mess."

"At least, I never left whiskers in the sink."

"No, but you always used my razor and then forgot to tell me, so I'd nearly cut my throat."

"I hardly ever used your crummy old razor! Why don't we talk about the way you left wet towels all over the bathroom? Or how you always used up the last of the soap and not tell me?"

She stepped back but not from anger. The twinkle in her eye told him she was enjoying this.

"You never made the bed once," he continued.

"You put your dirty socks on the floor instead of in the hamper," she countered teasingly.

"I hardly ever wore socks!"

"And when you did wear them, you never put them in the hamper!"

"At least I never forgot to unplug the curling iron. Do you know how many times I almost burned myself?"

"I always made sure the refrigerator door was securely closed and you always forgot to close it all the way," Chloe remembered as if it was yesterday.

"Considering you couldn't cook I'm surprised you knew what a refrigerator was!"

Chloe narrowed her eyes as she thought long and hard. "You used my eyebrow pencil to sketch."

"It's not as if you don't get them free. Besides, I couldn't find my drawing pencils at the time," he excused himself.

"And to think I felt guilty that I gave away that ugly blue flannel shirt."

Dalton's jaw dropped in shock. "You gave away my lucky shirt?"

Chloe placed one foot behind the other and slowly backed away. She knew she was in trouble. "It was just a shirt, Dalton."

"Just a shirt?" He advanced on her with the same rate as she retreated. "That wasn't just any shirt. That was the one I wore when I began every important piece. That shirt never let me down. And you gave it away?"

"It had holes in it."

"It had character!"

She quickened her retreat as he drew closer. "At least I didn't cut it up or anything. I just put it in a bag for charity. Are you really mad, Dalton?"

"No, I'm not angry," he said in a dangerous tone that boded ill for her. "I'm past mad. Do you know what I'm going to do to you?"

A nervous giggle escaped her lips.

"No." She almost tripped as she looked over her shoulder to make sure she still had a clear path.

He kept advancing. "Once I catch you, I'm going to..." He suddenly sped up and grasped her around the waist. She squealed in mock terror as he swung her around in a circle. "Tickle you!"

Chloe screamed in laughter as Dalton found her vulnerable spots. She twisted in his arms until she overbalanced the two of them and they fell to the sand, still laughing. They both lay back, looking up at the sky, feeling freer than they had in a long time.

"You know, some people pay therapists for what we just went through for free," he remarked.

Chloe remained quiet for a moment, savoring the closeness they shared. A closeness she couldn't remember them having even when they were married.

"Did you really hate my using your toothpaste?"

Dalton's shoulders shook with his laughter. He rolled over and buried his face against her neck, still laughing so hard she couldn't help but join in as he rubbed his bristly chin against her.

Their time for healing had begun.

CHLOE WRINKLED HER NOSE with distaste at the sight of crackers and coconuts for dinner, but she accepted her meal with good grace.

"It's a shame the raft didn't have oars," she commented, biting down on her cracker. "We could push it when the tide goes out and make our way around the other side of the island. Maybe we'd see other islands. We both believe the resort can't be all that far from here. Maybe we'd find it."

"It's risky, Chloe." He chose his words carefully. He didn't feel it was time to tell her the truth. "Once we got around to the other side of the island we might not see another even close by. And we might not be able to get back here."

"But we haven't even seen a ship in the distance," she remarked, starting to feel a little desperate. Even if the time alone with Dalton was heaven on earth.

"We've only been here a couple days," he reminded her. "If there's a lot of islands out there a rescue team will probably search them all. We know we could be next."

Chloe leaned forward and brushed a stray lock of hair from his face. She squinted her eyes, studying him with a degree that proved unnerving to him.

"What?" he asked warily.

"I'm just trying to picture you with shorter hair." She sat forward on her knees and cupped her hands around his head.

"No, thank you." He reared back from her reach. "I like my hair the way it is."

"But you have a very handsome face. A masculine face that needs to be shown off more. The right haircut could do it." She threaded her fingers through the thick strands and pulled them away from his face. "You have a slight wave in it that could be styled by the right hairdresser. Oh, I know you tie it back most of the time, but I've never seen you with short hair."

"And you never will. Why don't you worry about your own hair. All you do is torture the curl out of it, and you look gorgeous when it's wild like it was that night at the restaurant."

"That was because I let my hairdresser have his way. Believe me, I won't give in to him again." She was uneasy with the directional switch. She lifted her hand and touched the braid that was already coming undone. She quickly discovered she wasn't as good braiding her hair as Dalton was. "All that hair around my face isn't professional."

"Who says?"

She opened her mouth and abruptly closed it as she realized she would be stating the name she sensed he wouldn't want to hear.

"I do."

He grinned. He knew what name she was going to say, but couldn't get angry about it. "Your nose just grew about an inch."

Chloe lifted her chin. "I've always felt that flyaway hair doesn't look good on an executive. Especially one with a cosmetics firm where she needs to look perfect all the time."

"Very good. Your nose grew another quarter inch."

She threw the rest of her cracker at him, furious it only bounced harmlessly off his chest.

"You refuse to cut yours. I won't let mine go natural."

"Sculptors are expected to have long hair. We have to look eccentric," he told her. "Which is what I did when I still had my blue flannel shirt."

"It was more a rag than a shirt."

"But it was mine." He shook his head, looking mournful. "It was like a security blanket."

"Oh, for heaven's sake, I'll buy you a dozen shirts!" she said, exasperated with his attempt at making her feel guilty. And succeeding. She sat back, folding her legs under her.

"They won't be the same." He tossed her cracker back into her lap.

Chloe picked up her cracker and turned it over between her hands. "I slept in it."

Dalton stilled. He wasn't sure he heard correctly. "What?"

"I slept in it." She looked up. "In the beginning I missed you so much that the ratty old shirt made me feel better. It smelled like you, but then your scent faded and I was angry with myself for keeping it around, so I got rid of it. I thought it would make things easier."

"Did it?"

She shook her head. "In the end, it only made me feel depressed because I had the shirt but not the man. That's when I gave it away. I'm sorry."

He covered her hands, forcing them to stop their fidgeting.

"Don't worry about it. Not if it made you feel better, even for a little while," he said quietly, lacing his fingers through hers. He gently pulled her over onto his lap. "Maybe we both need to look for new security blankets. Starting with each other." He forced himself not to react when he felt her stiffen in his embrace.

"Aren't we moving a little fast?"

"We moved even faster first time around."

Chloe wrinkled her nose. "I was afraid you thought I was easy."

"Hey, wait a minute, *you* were the one who seduced me back then," he teased. "I was just this poor guy who was dazzled by your—"

She hooted. "Poor guy? I don't think so!"

Dalton rocked her back and forth. "We had fun back then." His voice was soft with memories. He used his nose to nudge a lock of hair away from her ear.

She nodded. "Fisherman's Wharf at midnight."

"Coit Tower." He uttered a husky growl in her ear as he nibbled on her lobe. He inhaled the musky scent of her skin, a smell more arousing than when she wore perfume. "Now there was a night."

Her murmur was agreement to the memory of a kiss that they felt rocked the landmark building on its foundation. They both had been surprised when an earthquake hadn't begun in wake of the rocketing desire between them.

"I wish we had talked like this back then." She rested the back of her head against his collarbone.

"Do you think it would have made things different?"

Her shoulders rose and fell in a deep sigh. "Probably not, but we might have been able to make each other understand how we felt. Maybe, if I had listened with my heart instead of with my ears, I would have realized just what Amanda was trying to do to us." She turned her head, pressing a kiss against the warm skin. She then turned her body so she lay with her cheek resting against his chest. "And to think it took my calling the agency for all this to happen. Rachel couldn't have picked a better husband if she tried," Chloe teased.

If she hadn't had her ear against his chest, she wouldn't have noticed the abrupt change in his heart rhythm.

"Dalton?" She glanced upward and saw the tight, flexing movements of his jaw. "What's wrong? Because we ran into each other the way we did? It's not as if you did more than escort women as their husband." Her smile died. "That is all you did for Rachel, isn't it?"

"Chloe, I never worked for Rachel in that sense," he abruptly cut in.

She sat up. "You mean this job was your first." Her expectancy hurt.

He shook his head. "I mean that I don't live very far from the Harrington Agency and Rachel and I are friends."

"Friends?" she asked skeptically.

"Not that kind of friend, remember?" he explained. "I'm designing a statue for her office courtyard. I was hoping to have it finished for her thirtieth birthday, which will be upcoming in several months."

She looked puzzled. "Now I am really confused. How did this all come about?"

He took a deep breath as if this was his now or never time.

"I was there the night you came to see Rachel," he said quickly. "I was in the adjoining office."

Horror replaced confusion as she realized what he was saying. "You listened to Rachel and I talking?"

He nodded. "I was there to meet her for dinner. She explained she had a late-night appointment and wanted me to wait downstairs. When I saw you get out of the car, I knew you shouldn't see me. Believe me, the door between the two offices was supposed to remain closed, but I wanted to know why you were there. I also persuaded Rachel to let me meet with you as your husband."

"It was all a sham," she said to herself, pain shadowing her voice.

"Never a sham," he hastily corrected her. "I saw it as a chance for us to be together again. I never forgot you, Chloe. I only hoped you hadn't forgotten me, either." He reached out and grasped her hands, willing her to listen to him. "I saw it as a chance for both of us."

She shook her head, confused by everything she was hearing. "Why didn't you tell me?"

"If you'd known I hadn't come through regular channels, so to speak, you would have refused to have anything to do with me. I figured, given your situation, I would have had better luck."

"Luck? What luck?" she repeated numbly. "You lied to me."

"No, I didn't. I just didn't tell you all of the truth." He dared not think of what he'd seen earlier. "I'm officially on Rachel's books, because she wanted this as aboveboard as possible. Don't blame her, Chloe. I talked her into it. She was furious when she discovered I had eavesdropped on the two of you."

"All right, you didn't tell me all of the truth." She walked over to the other side of the small fire he had lit for their dinner and sat down on the sand. "But that doesn't excuse you from keeping so much from me. From the beginning of this, you knew more than you let on. So now I don't have to think of you running around town posing as a husband to any businesswoman who wants the artist type. Instead, you've been living near Rachel's office and..." Her voice trailed off as she recalled where Rachel's business was housed and what the surrounding neighborhood was like.

She thought of an area once filled with elegant mansions that were now offices and lofts. Not exactly the neighborhood a starving artist would be found in.

Her mouth dropped open as lightning bolts struck overhead.

"No one without money could live in that vicinity. Last I heard there wasn't one rental in the area." She jumped to her feet and backed off. "Which can only mean one thing." The cogs in her mind rolled fast and furious. She looked ready to commit murder.

"You con man, you are no starving artist!"

Chapter Eleven

"I don't have money," Dalton contested. "I don't have anything close to the wealth you have."

"You have a studio in an expensive neighborhood!"

"It's a loft and I was lucky to get a good deal on it."

"You own a loft. Not a studio, but a loft." Chloe laughed, although not a bit of humor echoed in the sound. "I don't think even one of Rachel's 'husbands' could afford property in that area unless they have another source of excellent income. Which means you must be very successful with your sculpture."

"I've had some moderate success overseas with my work," he acknowledged.

"Moderate success?"

"I do nicely."

"Give me a better hint than that. How much do your pieces sell for?"

He told her.

"Are we talking their rate of exchange or ours?"

"My agent keeps track of all of that."

"Your agent. Of course, you'd have an agent. All successful sculptors have one. Is there anything else you want to tell me? Maybe news about a big show in

London or Paris? Maybe a valued patron named Lucretia?''

"That's not fair, Chloe."

"*That's not fair?* What about all the bombshells you've laid on me today?" She shook her fist in the air. "You complain about something minor as the way I squeeze toothpaste, and next thing you bring up this!"

"Chloe, the two don't go together."

"In my mind they do." She pressed her fingertips against her forehead. "What I wouldn't give for two aspirin right about now," she muttered.

Dalton dug through the kit. He handed her a metal mug filled with water and two white tablets.

She quickly downed the pills.

"Thank you."

Dalton smiled. Even in the face of adversity, Chloe's manners were always impeccable. He wondered if she would lose it completely if he told her he considered her a joy to watch.

Knowing Chloe, he'd probably be lucky to walk away with one part of his body in working order.

"I just can't believe you!" Chloe didn't seem to run out of steam as she continued. "But then, what can I say when I'm talking about a man who believed the television remote control should have been surgically grafted to his hand!"

"Wait a minute, I found some pretty good programs by surfing the channels," he defended himself.

"Oh sure!"

Dalton jumped to his feet and, in true caveman fashion, hauled Chloe into his arms for a kiss that shook her all the way down to her toes. He knew that because he could feel all ten tootsies curve against his calves. He wasn't about to let her come up for air too soon for fear she'd continue her tirade. Not when she felt like flowing hot silk in his arms and tasted like sin. Her mouth opened willingly under the thrust of his tongue as he tasted her heady flavor again and again.

By the time he released her he was positive his face was blue from lack of air. The taste of her was like a drug in his system and, funny thing, oxygen didn't seem to matter right then.

Chloe's body melted against his. Her mouth was swollen and her lips shining and moist from their kisses while her deep amethyst eyes were cloudy with pleasure. As she moved against him, he could feel her erect nipples press against his chest. Which made him want a hell of a lot more than another kiss. He slid his hands under her top and covered her breasts, feeling them swell under his caress. He ran his fingers along the perimeter, slowly moving the circular motion inward until he reached her nipples. He didn't miss her pleased murmur when he gently twisted them between his fingers.

"I must say, Mr. James," she murmured in a husky voice, looking up at him with a passion-drenched gaze, "you do have a way with words."

"I figured we'd done enough talking and it was time for some action," he replied, keeping a tight hold on her. Just in case.

"Such as?"

"Such as this." He maneuvered her down onto the tarp. Within seconds, they were naked and Chloe was sprawled across Dalton's body, pressing kisses across his chest. "Yep, that's it."

"I should punish you," she murmured, raking her teeth across his hair-roughened skin. She ran her fingertips across his nipple, then laved the copper pebble with her tongue. She looked up at him under the cover of her eyelashes with a siren's gaze that raised his internal temperature a good fifty degrees.

He closed his eyes as he felt her hand travel down until her cool fingers closed around his erection. He gulped when he felt her lips caress his navel, then her tongue flicker across the indentation. He hissed a sharp curse when her lips moved farther down while her fingers performed magic. He was positive a pleasurable death was forthcoming.

"Believe me, I feel suitably punished."

IT TOOK A WHILE for Chloe to realize a few things. Such as who won the argument.

"You are a horrible man," she told him, lightly scratching her nails across his chest as if she intended to draw blood.

He winced and grabbed hold of her hand. "Me? You were the one who about blew me out of the water."

Chloe giggled. "I have an idea if we had been in the water, we would have surely drowned."

"Yeah, but think of the fun we would have had before we succumbed." His chest rose and fell in a steady rhythm as he lay back, wondering when he could remember the last time he'd felt this content. "Chloe, I know you're furious with me for deceiving you about my working for Rachel, but at the time I thought it was for a good cause."

She lifted her head from where it lay pillowed on his chest. "And what good cause is that?"

"Us."

The silence after his telling statement was deafening.

"We've talked about the past. Now we need to talk about the present and future," he told her.

Chloe sat up and reached for her top and bottoms, which Dalton had ripped into shorts. She looked down with a wry smile at her tattered outfit.

"If no one shows up pretty soon, our rescue could turn into an embarrassing event." She idly chipped away at her battered manicure and wrinkled her nose at broken nails and chapped hands. "How do we know it's just not the atmosphere that's turned us into sex-crazed maniacs?" she asked the question that Dalton had been dreading to hear.

"Meaning?"

"Think about it, Dalton. Look where we are." She waved her arms over her head in a semicircle.

He turned his head first one way, then the other.

"I'd say we're pretty lucky. We could have been shipwrecked at the South Pole. Given the clothing we wore when you slipped overboard, even sharing body heat wouldn't have saved us."

"This is not a joke!" She punched his arm, although she couldn't have hurt him if she wanted to. "We're marooned in the kind of location fantasies are made of. Blue sky, white beach, warm water, palm trees. It's idyllic here. What if we're giving in to the dream? What about when we return to reality?"

"What if we're giving in to what we've been feeling since that night in the restaurant?" he countered. "Tell me the truth, Chloe, how much thought have you given us since we divorced?"

She grimaced. "More than I'd care to admit. But we can't forget that six years have passed. We had gone on to make new lives for ourselves and I can't imagine you've been a virtual monk all these years." Even if she wished he had been.

He faced her squarely, forcing her to return his gaze. "Would it bother you if I said I hadn't lived the life of a saint?"

"It would probably bother me more if you said you had turned into one."

Dalton leaned forward and wrapped his hand around her nape, digging his fingers into her scalp.

"We can't go back and recapture those six years, Chloe," he said softly, "and we shouldn't have any regrets during that time. I think the years apart just helped get us to this point where we can talk freely to each other."

She tipped her head to one side, resting her cheek against his arm, feeling the heat of his skin and inhaling his warm musky scent mingled with the tangier aroma of salt from their short swim in the ocean.

"I just want to remind you that you already promised not to dump me when we got back to San Francisco," he told her. "I don't take rejection well."

Her hopes rose with his reminder. That meant he wanted to keep seeing her when they returned. Even if she wondered if that day would come.

"I can't imagine any woman dumping you," she teased.

"Yes, but the only woman who matters is you."

Chloe smiled. "I like to hear that. Tell me more."

And he did. With his warm, dark, velvet voice, Dalton wove an erotic fantasy that had Chloe almost whimpering with desire.

"What color sheets do you have on your bed?" he suddenly asked her.

She looked at him as if he'd suddenly lost his mind. "What do the color of my sheets have to do with this?"

"You'll see. Come on, tell me. What color?" he pressed.

She closed her eyes. "Green."

"Dark or light green?"

"Light. Mint green."

"Hm, mint. Cool and refreshing." He wrapped his other hand around her nape. By keeping his arms straight, she was unable to move closer to him. "What other colors would I find in your bedroom?"

She gazed at him blankly. "Colors? The walls are painted in what the decorator called Warm Lights, but I call it off-white. My comforter is mint-and-rose zigzags on a cream-colored background and has a matching mint dust ruffle. The throw pillows are one of each color."

He smiled as he continued using his thumbs to rub her neck in slow and easy circles. "Just like ice cream. Funny, I wouldn't have thought you'd go in for pastels, considering you always wear strong colors."

Chloe was finding it more and more difficult to think under Dalton's ministrations. "I find them calming after a long day at the office."

"What else is in your bedroom besides a bed and dresser?"

She was convinced no one had as seductive a voice as Dalton's. Not dark velvet. It had a slightly rough quality to it that had her thinking of raw silk. How many times had she listened to his voice and thought about getting him alone?

"There's a painting over the bed. The usual multicolored swirls in colors to echo the comforter. Bookshelves. A linen chest at the foot of the bed. A vanity table. Nothing all that interesting." She wondered what he was getting at.

"What about when you're in bed? Do you just use it to sleep in or do you lie there and read or watch TV or listen to the radio?" he inquired.

"A little of each," she admitted, feeling the warmth steal up her body. And all he'd touched was her neck! "It's my escape room."

"Do you still wear those sexy silky little nothing nightgowns to bed?" he asked huskily. "The ones you refused to bring on the cruise."

"Yes." Her voice turned breathy with need. And here she'd made love with him a bare fifteen minutes before and she wanted him again!

"I wish you had brought them with you on the trip."

"Pajamas are more comfortable for traveling."

Dalton's smile was a hammer blow to Chloe's senses. How could she have thought she could live the rest of her life without seeing that megawatt smile of his? How many nights had his smile wrapped around her like a warm blanket when she came home from a bad day at the office? How many days had life brightened up just because he smiled at her?

"Not necessarily."

More importantly, how had she survived the past six years without that smile?

"Dalton," she whispered.

He shook his head. He dropped one hand to her shoulder, rubbing in the same seductive circular motion.

"What color nightgown would you be wearing?"

She closed her eyes. "Blue or red. Maybe black."

His voice dropped in pitch until it was like black raw silk.

"Let's go with the red. A hot contrast to the cool colors of the sheets. As if you aren't sure what you want to be. Which do you prefer?" he whispered. "The wild heat or serene coolness?"

"Something else you think we should discuss?" she asked, slightly shifting her body in the same direction his fingers took.

"I like to visualize where you're sleeping."

"Afraid you won't see it for yourself?" she softly taunted.

"Afraid that once you're back with the good Dame Amanda you'll decide to let her handle things again and I'll be nothing more than another bad memory."

Chloe opened her eyes. The amethyst depths were almost chilling.

"Don't ruin the mood, Dalton. And if you're going to play games, we'll do it both ways. If you hope to see my bedroom, I'll expect to see yours. Tell me the color of your sheets."

"The sheets are usually whatever I happen to have clean. I think the ones on the bed now are a dark blue-and-black print."

She placed her palm against his chest, feeling the heat of his skin. "King-size bed?"

"Is there any other kind?"

"Is it covered with plaster dust? I can think of many nights you'd be so tired you didn't take a shower. Maybe that's why sleeping here on the sand wasn't all that difficult to do."

"I won't be doing that after what I've gone through the past couple of days," he said readily. "After a couple nights sleeping on the tarp, I've come to realize just how uncomfortable sleeping on a gritty surface can be. And itchy," he added as an afterthought.

Chloe looked up and realized the sun was moving westward.

"Another day without a rescue," she said. "Do you think anyone will ever show up to save us? I can't understand why someone hasn't seen our fire. Thanks to the wind blowing the smoke out to sea, someone should have seen it by now."

"Hard to say." He was getting uneasy with this direction of their conversation. He suspected if Chloe found out he knew the resort was on the other side of the island he'd be dead meat, for sure. And she'd make it as painful as possible, too.

"I CAN'T DO IT!" Chloe wailed.

"Yes, you can," Dalton said firmly. "Just breathe in and out evenly and concentrate."

"This is not fun, Dalton!"

"Yes, it is, if you let it. Now try again." He walked over to her and arranged her arms and legs.

"It hurts," she said between her teeth.

"That's only because you're using muscles you normally don't use. Try again."

She stretched her leg out another quarter of an inch. "I seem to have been doing a lot of that lately."

"Trust me, you'll appreciate it in the end."

"I don't think so." Chloe winced as she lifted her arms in what she felt was an unnatural position. "Are you sure this will do something for me?"

"It will if you close your eyes, take even breaths and concentrate," he ordered.

"Slave driver." She complied by closing her eyes and slowing her breathing. Except, as before, her mind started to wander and she immediately lost her balance, falling back in the sand. "These martial-arts exercises or whatever you call them are stupid!" She slapped the sand with the flat of her hand.

Dalton was smart enough not to laugh as he walked over and held out his hand. Although he couldn't keep his lips from twitching with mirth.

Chloe glared at him, silently daring him to laugh. She slapped his hand away and stood on her own.

"I take an aerobics class three times a week," she told him. "I take a yoga class once a week. You have been doing this almost all your life. There is a big difference between the two and I think I'll stick with what I know best."

"You should be willing to try something new."

"Fine, when I get back home, I'll sign up for a weight-training class."

Dalton ignored her sarcasm.

"I'm going for a run up the beach. Wanna come along?"

She shook her head.

"I'm hot and sweaty and sticky." She grabbed her braid and shook it at him. "I'm going to head for that freshwater pool we found and take a swim."

"Why don't you wait until I get back from my run and we can go together?" he suggested, fearing she might get lost and wander onto the resort grounds.

Chloe's body heaved in a deep sigh. "I really wanted to go swimming now," she murmured with mock weariness. "But I'll wait. Just don't run for ten or twenty miles."

"Since I doubt the island is that large, I don't think you have to worry about my getting lost." He dropped a kiss on her lips, then lingered for more.

"Go." Chloe pushed him backward, but she was smiling. "We can pursue that idea after you get back."

He paused as if unsure he wanted that run now, but he turned and took off at an easy lope.

Chloe watched him until he was out of sight. She spread her legs in front of her and idly noticed her skin was turning the shade of golden toast. She had no idea she could tan as rapidly as she had. But then, considering the amount of time she spent outdoors, she wasn't surprised.

"Amanda is going to have hysterics when she sees this tan," she murmured, still looking at her legs. She was secretly pleased to see some color on her skin instead of what she always felt was pasty instead of porcelain. She examined her arms. "We really should think about adding a bronzing powder or cream to our line."

"NEXT TIME we come here, I suggest we bring a catered meal," Chloe said as they walked inland toward the waterfall and pool.

"Sounds good to me. And maybe I should pack the stereo, too," he went along with her fantasy. "Music would be a nice touch."

She looked at him, noting his cotton pants were rapidly becoming threadbare with the wear and tear they had endured. Looking at her own clothing, she realized her pajamas weren't faring much better.

"And no Maria," she said with mock severity.

He looked at her with innocence personified. "Maria who?"

She patted his cheek, then walked in front of him with a swing of the hips. "Good boy."

"Nah, I just don't want you mad at me again. The last time was more than enough."

Chloe shook her head. "I have never yelled at anyone in my life. Then, in the past few days, I've screamed and shrieked and generally sounded like a fishwife. I can't believe I could be so horrible." She looked over her shoulder. "You aren't going to argue with me on that point?"

"I thought we were past arguing."

She looked at him suspiciously. "You can't get out of it that easily. You might claim innocence, but I didn't miss the way Maria seemed to have an overflowing cleavage when you were around. Amazing how her buttons always managed to pop any time she saw you."

"Okay, so I noticed she had a good pair of lungs. Any man who was still alive would have noticed that." He pushed aside several large bushy leaves so she could pass by them. "But that doesn't mean I would want to take her up on her invitation. Not when I already have a hot woman around."

"Good thing." She spun around and grabbed hold of his pants waistband and pulled him toward her. "Just remember I do hand out horrible, scary punishments."

His eyes lit up with dark fires. "Oh, I remember, all right."

The moment they reached the glen, they didn't hesitate in shucking their clothing and diving into the water. Chloe loosened her braid and lay back to float on the water's surface while Dalton swam laps. She used her hands to paddle her way around the pool in slow, easy sweeps. The water was silky cool to her skin while the sun beat hotly down on her.

"How can you be so energetic after all that running you did?" she asked.

He slowed his strokes and swam over to her, settling for an easy sidestroke to keep pace with her. "The exercise helps me clear out any cobwebs. When I'm working, I tend to focus on my sculpture so much that the world kind of recedes. Exercise helps bring me back from that world."

She looked at him out of the corner of her eye. She wondered what he would say if she told him with his hair floating on the water and deeply tanned features, he resembled a pirate.

"And since you don't have your work right now, you at least have that to concentrate on."

He flashed her his pirate's grin as his eyes fastened on her breasts bobbing in the water. "Among other things, yes."

Chloe made the mistake of not thinking of where she was and lashed out at him. As she reached over to playfully punch him on the arm, she immediately flailed and sunk underwater. She bobbed up, sputtering.

"Not funny!" she choked.

Dalton shook his head in mute apology as he laughed. "But you look so cute when you resemble one of those ducks whose heads bob in a glass of water!"

"You're comparing me to a toy duck?" Her yell seemed to bounce off the trees as she attacked while he easily evaded her clumsy efforts in trying to drown him.

"Come on, Sumner, you can do better than that!" he mocked, swimming to the other side of the pool.

"You Neanderthal you." With a muttered curse, she struck out, only to screech when he suddenly dove underwater and grabbed hold of her legs, pulling her with him. She barely had enough warning to keep her mouth closed.

Dalton's idea of underwater swimming turned out to mean fastening his mouth on hers as they rose to the surface. Chloe linked her arms around his neck, hanging on for dear life as they treaded water.

"And what do you call that maneuver?" she asked huskily, wrapping her legs about his hips. She smiled as she felt his arousal nudge her.

"How about 'sink the submarine'?" he suggested with a wicked grin, only able to keep them afloat with the strength of his legs kicking out.

Chloe burst out laughing. "That is so juvenile, Dalton."

"Are you sure?" He thrust his hips forward.

She sucked in a breath as she felt his arousal nudge her center. She felt a heavy liquid warmth settle deep within her.

"No, I'd say this is strictly adult entertainment."

They were so intent on each other, the island could have sunk into the sea and they wouldn't have noticed.

Except, instead of the island sinking, faint voices sounded off in the distance. At that moment, they weren't aware of anything except each other.

"Ah, here we are!" a man's voice announced.

The scene seemed to unfold between both parties in slow motion.

Chloe's and Dalton's heads turned toward the intrusion the same time Nando stared at them with openmouthed shock.

"Chloe! Dalton!" he exclaimed, unaware of the several people behind him looking on with shocked amusement.

Chloe had no idea what to say. She settled for taking a deep breath and sinking down under the water.

"Nando, what a surprise." Dalton greeted the other man with calm composure. "Fancy meeting you here."

Chapter Twelve

"I cannot believe that all this time you were just on the other side of the island!" Nando had gallantly draped his polo shirt over Chloe's head once he'd seen the state her own clothing was in.

Once the initial shock had subsided, he dispatched his party to return to the resort. He waited, with his back turned, while Chloe and Dalton climbed out of the water and had gotten dressed. He looked at them with amazement as if he couldn't believe what he was seeing.

"We have been searching for you since that morning when we first discovered you were not on board," he told them. Chloe had haltingly explained she and Dalton had gone out on the deck for a breath of air and she had slipped overboard and he had dove over to save her. "We had no idea you were so close! We were afraid the raft had been carried farther out to sea, so our staff has been searching the other small islands in the vicinity and had put out a bulletin to any vessel in the area."

Chloe's lips trembled with her effort to keep her strained smile in place as Nando ushered her toward a waiting golf cart.

"Yes, well, we had no idea, either," she murmured, wondering if she would be able to look back on this episode and laugh about it. At this moment, she doubted that time would ever come.

Not that she minded being found in Dalton's arms. It was being found while they were naked and making love that sent her reeling.

She sat gingerly on the leather seat, almost flinching when Dalton sat next to her, his bare thigh brushing against hers.

"And here I only thought this happened in movies and books," he said under his breath.

"Don't say a word." She held herself erect for fear if she relaxed the least little bit she would shatter into a million pieces. "Not one word."

"How did you end up here?" Nando asked, looking over his shoulder as the driver took off.

"We have no idea." Dalton did the talking. At the moment, he felt it was safer. "I got Chloe into the raft and, at first, I was more worried about making sure she wasn't badly hurt. It wasn't until then I realized we had no way to contact you. The radio battery was shot. By the time we washed up on the beach, I was just grateful we hadn't drowned."

The other man shook his head, clucking under his tongue.

"You two were very lucky. I still cannot believe you were so close to us."

"Yes, amazing, isn't it?" Dalton kept his smile noncommittal.

Chloe looked around, noting the suddenly cleared vegetation and outer buildings. People, looking tanned and fit, instead of bedraggled like her, stared at them curiously as the cart rumbled past.

"I had your luggage placed in one of our bungalows set aside for our valued guests," Nando told
them. "I knew we would find you. I did not realize it
would be so easy." He smiled, then cast Chloe an
apologetic glance. "I am afraid I had not notified your
grandmother of your disappearance yet. I thought it
would only worry her when I felt we had an excellent
chance of finding you."

"True, she wouldn't need the stress," she agreed,
offering up a faint smile. She suddenly felt chilled and
huddled under the warmth of Nando's polo shirt. *Nor
would you want to lose the chance of making this deal
of a lifetime. A deal that wouldn't go through if
Amanda was furious with you for losing her only
granddaughter.*

The cart stopped in front of a small pink stuccoed
bungalow. Nando helped Chloe out and escorted the
couple to the door.

"If you'd like I can send over a maid," he offered,
handing Dalton the magnetic key card.

She immediately shook her head. "No, thank you.
I think I'd like to take a bath—" she felt her courage
start to slip at her choice of words "—and relax."

"Would it be possible to have dinner served here?"
Dalton asked.

Nando looked disappointed at his request. "I
thought we could meet for dinner and—"

Dalton swiftly cut him off. "The past several days
have been very stressful for Chloe. Right now she
needs rest more than anything."

Nando inclined his head. "Of course. Extension
eight will connect you with room service. They will
prepare anything you wish."

Chloe managed a smile that didn't reveal any of her tension. "Thank you, Nando." She held out her hand. "Perhaps we can meet in the morning and talk."

He picked up her hand and caressed the back with his lips. "I will be waiting for your call." He waited until she entered the room before turning to Dalton with an apologetic smile. "I am sorry we happened to barge in on an intimate moment."

Dalton shrugged. "It was just one of those things, Nando. Better you than a perfect stranger."

The other man flashed a brilliant smile. "The pool and waterfall is a romantic spot. I can understand why you wished to make use of it." With a wave of his hand he walked back to the waiting golf cart.

Dalton took a deep breath before walking into the bungalow.

"Back to reality."

He cocked his head to one side as he heard the sound of the shower running and figured out where Chloe had headed the first moment she could. He wandered through the sitting room and bedroom until he reached the bathroom.

"Don't use all the hot water!" he shouted from the doorway. He crossed his arms in front of his chest as he leaned against the doorjamb, intent on enjoying the view of her naked body partly obscured by steam and frosted glass.

"I'm not leaving here until I am clean!" she shouted back.

Dalton straightened up and his hands went to his pants waistband as he walked toward the shower. "Then I guess there's only one thing to do if I want any of that hot water."

He shucked his pants and tossed them to one side while pulling open the shower door.

Chloe's look of outrage was comical. "This is my shower, buster. You can wait your turn." She tried to reach past him for the door, but he stepped in before she had a chance to shut him out.

"Hey, you're not the only one who needs to get off the sand," he reminded her, blithely taking the soap out of her hand. He lifted the pale pink bar to his nose and sniffed. "Isn't there a soap that has a more masculine smell to it?" He shrugged and began soaping his chest. "Still, I guess if this is Bella Skin's product, it has to be good. What do you think it sells for? Fifty dollars a bar?" He wrinkled his nose at the feminine floral scent that drifted from the creamy soap.

Chloe tipped her head back, narrowing her eyes against the spray of water. "I was here first. You can wait your turn."

"What are you worried about? It's not as if we haven't shared a bath before." His teeth flashed white in his face. "So to speak."

"It still wouldn't hurt you to wait until I finish." Her face was free of all expression.

Except Dalton wasn't going to let her shut him out. Not after what they had shared the past few days.

He realized they both had also gone through an emotional roller coaster and sensed Chloe wasn't handling all this upheaval well. Her body was stiff in his arms instead of soft and yielding as it had been at the pool. He sensed she was embarrassed over what had happened.

"Chloe," he said gently, taking her chin between his fingers and tipping it upward. "No one really saw anything."

A soft moan escaped her lips. "Oh, right, you and I were naked in a pool of water that was like clear glass. Not only were we naked, we were . . . were . . ." She uttered a soft scream of frustration as she grabbed the bar of soap out of his hand and threw it at his chest.

"Wait a minute!" Dalton grabbed hold of her hands and held them up between them. "Chloe, you're on the verge of losing it. You need to calm down."

"Calm down my foot! What I need to do is turn back the past few days and get my life together again!" She jerked her hands free and turned away from him.

Dalton took that moment to bend over and pick up the bar of soap, setting it back in the soap dish. "You're upset because of what happened back at the pool and I understand your worries, but you're letting it get all out of proportion. All along, you've been afraid we wouldn't get rescued. Well, guess what, we did! And all of a sudden, I don't have the south seas nymph I was shipwrecked with!"

Chloe whipped around so fast her hair swung around and slapped her in the face. She pushed the sodden mess out of the way.

"That kind of statement is something only a man would say."

"Why is it our sex always gets blamed when we state a logical conclusion?" he asked, starting to feel more than a little frustrated with the way she was acting.

"Because the last thing I want to hear is anything logical!" she wailed.

Dalton looked down at her face and saw the misery he remembered seeing when she first realized they were stranded on the island. He folded her in his arms, stepping in front of the spray so her face was protected.

"You've been through a lot this past week, haven't you?" he murmured. "No wonder you're not sure whether to scream or cry. Maybe you need some chocolate to calm down."

"Don't you dare patronize me!" She dug her fist into his abdomen.

He nimbly stepped out of the way before she caused further damage. "No, I'm trying to force you to calm down." Seeing a hug wasn't going to help, he spun her around and began massaging her neck. He used his thumbs to loosen the knots of tension along the top of her back.

"How can I have a business meeting with the man after he's seen me naked?" she moaned, tipping her chin against her chest.

"Sweetheart, he saw more of me naked than he saw you," he crooned.

His assurance only caused her more anxiety. She muttered several curses under her breath.

"And you thought that would make me feel better?"

"Well, I hoped." He retrieved the soap and rubbed it between his palms until they were covered with lather. Then he stroked his hands down her back. "Now inhale deeply and hold your breath for a second," he directed, waiting until she complied. "Now do it again. No, not so fast or you'll hyperventilate. That's it. Slow and easy." As he soaped her body in lingering strokes, he continued speaking in a low voice designed to soothe the spirit. While he would have liked to try something more athletic, he knew Chloe needed love and comfort. By the time he finished, she was half-asleep. He got her out of the shower and dried her off before carrying her to the bed. He whipped the aqua-and-pink bedspread off before laying her down on the soft aqua sheets. She murmured a few unintelligible words, rolled over onto the pillow and promptly fell asleep.

Dalton stared down at her slumbering figure.

"She'll complain about going to sleep with wet hair and she'll be furious with me for turning her into a zombie," he murmured, pulling the sheet up and draping it around her shoulders. "But I'm hoping she'll wake up as that wild woman I love."

CHLOE WOKE UP feeling as if she'd been drugged. She opened her eyes a slit, then closed them again.

"It's a dream," she muttered. "Just a dream. The next time I open my eyes I'll see the sand and water."

"Do you want to call this a dream?" a masculine voice crooned in her ear.

Her nostrils flared at the aroma floating up her senses.

"It's not a dream. It's a nightmare and I'm fantasizing that I smell a steak."

"Try again, sweetheart."

Her eyes popped open and looked down at the small plate Dalton held in front of her. But it wasn't the fine china that interested her. It was the contents.

"*Yes!*" She grabbed one of the chocolate pieces and stuffed it in her mouth. And moaned with pleasure as the rich taste exploded in her mouth.

"And here I thought I was the only one who could give you that kind of satisfaction," he said wryly, sitting on the edge of the bed.

Chloe sat up, oblivious to her nudity as she reached for the plate.

"Uh-uh." He held it out of her reach and held up the other plate. "Steak first, then you can have dessert."

She stared at the transformation sitting before her. While she slept, Dalton had finished his shower, washed his hair and shaved. The uncivilized pirate she remembered was gone. She briefly mourned his passing. He was dressed in a white cotton shirt and jeans. She would have bet he was also barefoot.

"Room service is very prompt here," he told her. "For a spa, no one said anything when I ordered a couple of steaks with baked potatoes."

He set the plates down on the bed and walked over to the closet where their clothes had been hung up. Chloe surmised the maid had unpacked for them after Nando arrived at the island. He brought back her robe and handed it to her.

"A heavy meal like this is probably not good for us, considering the little food we've had, but I couldn't resist." He picked up the plates and carried them back into the sitting room.

Chloe pulled on her robe and followed him. She muttered a curse when she felt the tangled hair hugging her neck.

"I have an idea I'm going to give their beauty salon a real challenge tomorrow," she said, walking into the sitting room. "My hair is such a disaster I'll be very surprised if they can do anything short of shaving my head."

"I don't think they'll go that far," he assured her.

She murmured her pleasure when she found a linen-covered table set with their meal. Dalton pulled out her chair for her, and when he pushed her forward he dropped a kiss on top of her head.

"Think anyone would notice if we locked the door and kept to ourselves for, say, a month or so?"

"I thought you wanted to concentrate on food," she teased, picking up her knife and fork.

"That's what room service is for. They can leave the trays outside the door."

Her mouth watered as she stared at the food. "Amazing a health spa would serve such rich food when people are coming here to lose weight." She eyed the butter-laden baked potato.

"I don't think this is the kind of health spa we're familiar with," Dalton said, pouring wine into her glass, then his own, before he sat down to her left. "While you had your nap, I looked over the various brochures on the writing desk. The resort offers any beauty service you can imagine, along with tennis, golf, swimming and a variety of exercise classes only if you're in the mood to move your body. They have a doctor and nurse on duty at all times. Guests who desire complete privacy are put in their West Pavilion. I think that's where we are. It's a series of bungalows that have secluded patios for private sunbathing and include staff members on twenty-four-hour call. They have lectures in the main building during the day and offer dancing in the evenings. I'd call this place a playground for the wealthy."

Chloe glanced at the crystal clock set on the table and realized she'd slept more than four hours.

"You've been busy," she commented.

"I was curious about the place and decided a little research wouldn't hurt." He dug in hungrily.

Silence reigned as they gave in to their hunger and ate. Chloe was careful to eat slowly, stopping when she felt full. She was stunned to watch Dalton not stop until his plate was squeaky clean.

"I was hungry," he defended himself.

"Hungry? You practically inhaled your food!"

He held up his hands in a "look at me" gesture. "I need to keep up my energy."

Chloe wrinkled her nose at his none too subtle teasing.

"There was a time when you had such a way with words."

"Yes, I remember you telling me that once." His husky voice reminded her of the time when she said the same sentence, and what happened afterward. He smiled as he watched her smother a yawn. "Looks as if you're ready for another nap."

"I can't be!" she protested, fighting another yawn.

"Considering the past few days it's not surprising. Maybe you'd prefer relaxing in the tub first." A hot light entered his eyes. "This bathroom outdoes the one on the yacht."

Chloe looked at the serving table. "No dessert?"

Dalton grinned at her hopeful tone. "Would chocolate mousse make things all better?"

"Where?"

Her eyes widened as he reached for two crystal dessert goblets filled with a rich creamy chocolate confection topped with a rosette of whipped cream decorating the top and chocolate shavings sprinkled on top of that.

"I figured if anything would make your day this would do it," he told her, placing one of the goblets in front of her. "I told room service that we needed something smooth, rich and chocolate to make up for our hardship. This was the recommendation.''

Chloe dipped her spoon into the thick mixture and slowly lifted it to her lips. She moaned appreciatively as the rich chocolate flavor slid down her throat.

"I guess you approve," Dalton murmured, more intent on watching her than eating his own dessert.

"Mmm," she crooned, dipping her spoon in again. She glanced at him. "Aren't you going to eat yours?"

"I think I'll enjoy watching you eat more."

Smiling, Chloe scooped her spoon into the mousse and lifted it in Dalton's direction.

"Then I'll share with you," she said huskily, tapping the end of the spoon against his lips. He obediently opened his mouth and swallowed the treat.

"I admit it does taste better that way," he murmured.

She smiled smugly. "Of course, it does." She took a bit of mousse for herself, then gave him the next spoonful. When her dish was empty, Dalton dipped his spoon into his dish and offered the same service to Chloe.

"With you, chocolate has taken on a whole new meaning." He tapped the spoon against her nose and leaned over and licked the confection off. He looked back at the goblet with a considering gaze, then up at Chloe.

"Don't even think about it," she warned, easily reading the direction of his thoughts. "I hate to think what housekeeping would think of us if we asked for clean sheets because we got chocolate all over the ones we have!"

"It was a thought."

"We'll just keep it that way," she said firmly, standing. The moment she got to her feet, weariness overtook her with a huge wave and she swayed a bit.

"Thought so." Dalton hurried to her side and swept her up in his arms.

Chloe draped her arms around his neck as he carried her back into the bedroom.

"This isn't how I imagined tonight," he gently teased her as he laid her back on the bed.

She yawned. "Neither did I," she murmured sleepily even as she succumbed to her weariness.

THE NEXT MORNING, Chloe didn't waste any time in setting appointments with the resort's beauty salon for her hair and a facial. Since Dalton was at the health club sparring with one of the instructors who taught martial arts, she didn't feel as if she was abandoning him.

"Such beautiful hair," the stylist told her as she washed and added a deep conditioner to her hair. "Why do you want me to apply those horrible chemicals to straighten it?"

"Because it would be easier to keep it out of my face," she replied, closing her eyes as the woman massaged her scalp with strong fingers.

"Then why not cut it?"

Chloe thought for a moment. "I had considered that."

"You have lovely features for a shorter cut. If you'd allow me to show you."

She deliberately ignored Dalton's insistence she not cut her hair. "Yes."

"When I finish you will look even more beautiful."

A couple hours later, Chloe looked at a total stranger.

Her hair had been cut short and sassy—the hairdresser's words—with curls around her face, but in a more controlled manner. Her tanned skin had been softened with mud packs and exotically scented creams and left with a glow she sensed wasn't just due to the facial treatments.

Realizing her cosmetics weren't right for her darker skin tone, she purchased new eye makeup and lipsticks. Then, as if that wasn't enough, she visited the resort's boutique and chose several new outfits that complemented the new her.

"If Amanda saw me, she would faint," she murmured, catching a glimpse of herself in the mirror. She had already changed into the one-piece soft cotton shorts outfit. The bright turquoise was accented with hot pink—two colors she had never even dreamed of wearing before. Even her sandals, which were only a few strategic straps were a bright pink leather to match her outfit. She jammed on a hot pink billed cap over her curls and set out for the bungalow.

As she walked along she glanced toward the tennis courts and swimming pool. For the moment, neither activity appealed to her. For now, she'd settle for finishing her business and returning to San Francisco. And seeing how she and Dalton would function once back in their old lives.

No, that was wrong, she reminded herself. The beginning of a new life.

"Wait a minute, I know those sexy legs." A male voice declared coming up from behind.

Chloe squealed when a pair of arms snaked around her waist and swung her in a half circle.

Dalton reared back when he stared at her face. For a moment, hot desire flared from his eyes. Then something else took over. He put her down and snatched off the hat.

"What the hell happened to your hair?" he roared, watching her curls spring into a feminine disorder.

She looked around, praying no one heard him. "Dalton, please."

He kept her cap out of her reach. "You cut it." He looked as if she had mortally wounded him.

"It was a mess. It was necessary," she lied.

He shook his head. "You didn't have to cut it and we both know it. Why?"

"Because I wanted something new and this was the best way to start it." She snatched back her cap and jammed it back on her head. "Now don't say another word."

He stepped back and looked her over from head to foot. "Actually, the rest of you looks great."

"Good, remember that." She picked up her packages that had dropped when he had grabbed her. "Nando and I have a meeting in a half hour." She glanced at the women lounging by the pool. A good number of them were eyeing Dalton with a great deal of interest. Most of them were sunbathing topless. "Dalton."

He smiled back in an inquiring way.

Chloe fixed a stern look on her face. "Stay away from the pool."

Chapter Thirteen

"I hope you have recovered from your ordeal with no ill effects," Nando greeted Chloe as she entered the office conference room set aside for their use. "I must say you look very lovely, *cara*. Your new hairstyle is very becoming. Short hair suits you. It makes you look very tempestuous, fiery and passionate."

Instead of changing into more businesslike clothing, Chloe had kept her brightly covered shorts suit on even if, she noticed with amusement, her briefcase didn't go with the outfit. For a moment she wondered if her choice of clothing was a mistake.

"Thank you, I feel more like myself. Although the hairstylist called my new cut sassy." She smiled back, placing her briefcase on the table. "And now that I've had all this relaxation time I see no reason why we can't hammer out the last few details in record time, do you? And I'm counting on you to give me a tour of the resort. What little I've seen is very impressive."

Nando uttered a theatrical groan. "And here I thought you would be too weak to think coherently. No wonder I was attracted to you from the beginning."

"Sorry, Nando," she said without a hint of apology. "I want to remind you I'm already taken."

"Ah, but you haven't been with me yet. As for our talk, I would have hated winning all the points if it was only because you were not working at your usual best." He waited as a secretary carried in a tray and deposited cups of coffee in front of them. He offered the young woman a dazzling smile and turned back to Chloe. "But then, I would only recommend we continue our discussion at my bungalow."

"Right here is just fine," she said crisply. *Where was the man she had dealt with on the yacht? Why the shift after he finally admitted she was taken and there would be nothing between them but friendship.* "Shall we begin?"

The expression in his eyes was boiling hot. "Oh, yes."

As THE BALANCE of the morning passed, Chloe soon began to realize a few things. Nando had obviously done a great deal of homework during her absence and was prepared to fight hard for even the smallest of details.

She also realized her mind wasn't as focused on business as it should have been. For brief seconds she thought of the beautiful day outside and how nice it would be to be out there, enjoying the sunshine with Dalton.

She was unsettled by this lack of concentration and forced herself back to the issues before her.

"You have to understand that the Sumner women aren't meant to have a man in their lives full time." Amanda's voice echoed in her mind. *"But that doesn't*

stop us from having liaisons when the time is appropriate.''

No, Amanda, it doesn't have to be that way. The thought suddenly popped into her head.

"Cara?" Nando looked at her questioningly.

"This coffee is delicious," she said brightly, reaching for her cup and sipping it. Truthfully, she hadn't taken any yet.

"You have changed," he mused, studying her carefully.

"Oh?" She drank her coffee until the cup was empty and immediately reached for the carafe.

His dark eyes scanned her face with an alarming intensity.

"You have become even more beautiful. Skin as delicate as rare porcelain is now the shade of rich gold," he said huskily, leaning toward her. "Your eyes shine like the most precious of jewels."

"We have very little left to go over, Nando," she reminded him, not liking the direction the discussion was going.

"I have never seen you look more incredible," he continued. "You fire my blood."

Chloe pressed her lips tightly together before she burst into laughter.

"Nando, we're getting off subject here."

He went on in his rich, accented rumble. "Don't you realize how much I desire you?"

"I thought we settled that problem on the *Bella*." She was beginning to feel a little frantic.

He stood and walked around to her side of the table. "That was before I saw this new side of you. You have no idea how beautiful you looked in the pool with the waterfall in the background. You were an exotic flower out there. A beauty among the jungle.''

Chloe feared if she wasn't fast she would lose all control of the discussion.

''Why don't we discuss those delivery dates again?'' she suggested.

''I'd rather discuss you.'' He grasped her by the shoulders and lifted her out of her chair.

''The subject of me isn't on the table.'' She realized what was happening and feared it would take an outright insult to get him to back off.

He started to lean forward so she had no choice but to lean back with her hips resting against the table rim.

''You should be.'' His lips pursed ready for a kiss. ''I must taste you. I want to see if you are as passionate as you look.''

''I don't think so.'' She ducked under his arm and made her way around the table toward the door. Her hand barely covered the knob before he reached her.

''Darling!''

Chloe was growing alarmed at this new side of Nando. She spun around, keeping her back to the door and her hand on the knob, carefully twisting it.

''Dalton is waiting for me,'' she carefully enunciated. ''Dalton, my husband.''

His face lowered to hers. ''You can't tell me he can give you the passion you truly deserve,'' he whispered huskily. ''I have talked to your Dalton, my darling. He doesn't have what you need.''

''He has plenty.''

''Does he?'' He pressed even closer.

Chloe's hand slipped off the doorknob and she blindly reached for it again. She was afraid if she didn't get out of there fast the situation could become dangerous. Not that she was afraid for herself. But that it could prove embarrassing to both of them.

"Perhaps we should take a break for lunch and continue this later this afternoon?" she smoothly suggested.

His face was so close to hers, she could feel his hot breath on her cheek.

"I had no idea you were such a golden goddess," he said with a fervency that could have been alarming. "I thought you were unreachable, so pale, so lovely. And now I see how full of fire you truly are." His lips blindly reached for hers.

Chloe dodged his kiss and twisted the doorknob at the same time.

"We really need to—" At the same time, she started to turn the knob, the door opened from the other side. Since Chloe had bent her body backward to evade Nando, her balance was off and she fell with him on top of her. Her shriek of surprise was muffled by his body. Her scream was cut off as she looked up at the rapidly darkening expression on Dalton's face.

"Did I interrupt something?"

Nando stumbled to his feet and reached down to get Chloe. She ignored his outstretched hand and looked up at Dalton. She saw no help there. She stumbled to her feet on her own. She looked around, grateful there was no one else in the hallway to see a position that could have been construed compromising.

"We have nothing to apologize for, Dalton. You have to realize your wife has fired my desire," Nando explained without a trace of embarrassment. "Naturally, I would follow that desire."

Chloe could have cheerfully choked the man.

Dalton looked as if he wanted to kill him. With his bare hands.

"You son of a bitch," he bit out each word with stark precision.

"Dalton!" While she wanted to kill Nando herself, she didn't think it was a good idea to insult him. Not as long as the merger hadn't been finalized yet.

He turned on her next. "What did you say to him?"

Her anger was rapidly turning into white-hot fury. There was no way she'd allow him to blame her for this. "Nothing."

Dalton's gaze raked her down to her toes. It was as if he was making sure she was still in one piece. He turned back to Nando. Before anyone could utter a word, his hands shot forward and grasped the front of Nando's shirt. The man had to stand on his toes so he wouldn't strangle from the tight hold.

"If you ever try to touch my wife again, I will reach inside your chest and rip out your heart," Dalton said in a conversational tone as if he was talking about nothing more important than the weather. "Do you understand me?"

Nando's eyes bulged as he gurgled out the word, "Yes."

Dalton released him. "Good." He turned to Chloe, who watched him the way a rabbit eyed a coyote. "Let's get some lunch." He took her arm and guided her down the hallway.

"What the hell do you think you're doing?" She released her fury the moment she knew they were alone. She glared at his back, wishing she had a knife to bury in it.

"What did it look like?" He didn't look right or left as they marched toward the main door.

"You acted like something out of the caveman era back there. I am conducting a business deal with that man and your actions could have ruined the entire association!" She found it difficult to keep her voice soft when all she wanted to do was scream at him. She briefly thought of the times she'd yelled on the beach. She wished for five minutes of that time again.

Dalton stopped so abruptly Chloe ran into his back.

"It wasn't difficult to figure out he had his hands all over you."

"He did not!"

"It sure as hell looked like it!"

Chloe made shushing noises as she looked around. "Nothing happened," she whispered fiercely. "Nando seemed to think I'd suddenly turned into some jungle goddess or something. He started to get a little out of hand and I was diffusing the situation by suggesting we adjourn for lunch when you barged in and—"

"Barged in? The secretary told me to go on in." He leaned over, deliberately putting his face in hers. "I wouldn't have cared if the man was the president of the United States. All that mattered to me was that I saw him putting his hands on my wife and I intended to protect her."

"You can't do that when there's a business deal involved," she argued.

"I will if my wife is involved. And you sure as hell didn't look as if you appreciated his attention." He stabbed the air with his forefinger.

Chloe saw red. How dare Dalton treat her like this? Why couldn't he remember she was a more than competent businesswoman? Who was he to treat her this way?

"Then you have nothing to worry about since you should remember you haven't been my husband for the past six years," she retorted. "You were back with me for this trip. That's all."

"Yeah, and you were willing to hire someone for it, weren't you?" he shot back.

The moment the words left her mouth, she looked up to see Nando standing behind Dalton. The triumph in his eyes told her there was no doubt he had heard every word she spoke.

"I hate men," she spat out before turning on her heel and stalking out. The ornate glass doors almost shattered in her wake.

"You didn't reconcile?" Nando asked Dalton with great interest.

He glared at their host. "I suggest you forget that because she is still my wife, whether she wants to admit it or not."

Nando held up his hands in surrender. "I have no excuse. I was carried away by the new glow in darling Chloe's face. You understand these things."

"The woman is married and off-limits." Dalton took a deep breath. "I'd like to punch your lights out, Nando, but she'd probably kill me for it."

Nando smiled. "This will not ruin our deal together. Working with Chrysalis Cosmetics will be an excellent advantage for Bella Skin. But I will push for a few points in our favor now."

Dalton shook his head. "I still want to hate your guts, but you don't let me."

He shrugged. "It's my Italian lover upbringing. My father was a famous lover. I must keep up the image. But I would like to know more about the two of you no longer being married."

"Forget it." Realizing he had a dangerous situation to diffuse, Dalton sprinted off after Chloe. In order to make it back to the bungalow before her he took a path he'd remembered seeing when he first saw the resort.

By the time he reached the door, he had enough time to get inside before she entered.

"You!" She slammed the door after her. "How did you get back here so fast?"

"I took the shortcut behind the tennis courts." He watched her stalk toward the bedroom. "Chloe, we need to talk."

"We have nothing to say." She threw open the closet doors and pulled out shirts and pants.

Dalton watched her toss his clothing on the bed. "I won't let you kick me out again without our talking about it."

"You did more than enough talking back there. After what happened, we will lose some very important points in this negotiation."

"How do you know that?"

"Because you forced me to announce we are no longer married!" Her words bounced off the walls.

"Forced you? I did what any red-blooded man did. I protected what's mine. Okay, so some would consider it Neanderthal, but I won't allow any male to manhandle my woman."

"But I'm not yours!"

"Yes, you are!"

Chloe reached inside the closet and pulled out his carryall. She dumped his clothing inside without bothering to fold them first.

"It is going to take everything I have to save this deal. And in order to do it, I don't intend for you to be here to ruin it,'' she stated. "A helicopter will fly you to Honolulu where you can take a plane. I'll arrange your return transportation for you."

He crossed his arms in front of him. "I am not going anywhere."

Chloe dropped the shirt she still held on the bed. "It's for the best, Dalton." She lowered her voice to a cajoling tone. "I'm going to be busy with damage control here. It might be best if you weren't around to remind Nando he was made a fool of."

Dalton couldn't remember ever feeling as angry as he did just then.

"Me remind him? You were the one who was going to hire a perfect stranger to pretend to be your husband, so Nando would keep his hands off of you," he argued. "It sure didn't seem to help, did it? Although—" he tapped his finger against his chin as he considered something "—you have to think about why he suddenly turned into a maniac. It wasn't just the way you look or that you're dressing sexier. It's the fact that you've been indulging in some pretty hot sex for the past few days." He smiled at her as if he just uttered an important formula.

Chloe's eyes bulged out of their sockets. "You conceited rat," she stormed. "You low-down sneaking male. Is that what you told him?" She advanced on him with murder on her mind.

He didn't budge an inch. "I didn't have to. He caught us at the pool, remember?"

"You told me he didn't see anything!"

"I lied."

Chloe, who never lost her temper or raised her voice, looked around for something she could throw at Dalton. And after she threw the contents of the room, she intended to tear him into tiny pieces with her hands.

As the rage built up within her, she realized she couldn't remain in the same room with Dalton. Not without killing him.

"Then that means you lied about a lot of things. You lied when you said you could handle anything that had to do with my work and we would be able to discuss our thoughts in a rational manner." She settled for picking up her pink cap and settling it on her head. "Do us both a favor and take the helicopter." She started to walk out of the room, then paused as if something occurred to her. "You said you took a shortcut behind the tennis courts. How did you know one was there?"

He shrugged. "I saw it when I found the resort a couple days ago..." His voice drifted off as he realized he'd made a major mistake. He didn't have to see the fire in her eyes to know she picked up on it. "I meant to tell you about that," he said calmly as he faced her.

"Tell me what?" she asked between clenched teeth.

"That the one day I was looking around I saw the resort."

"The day I asked you if you'd seen anything and you told me *no?*"

He knew he was in trouble now. "I didn't actually say no. So I didn't really lie to you."

Chloe swallowed several times. Her anger was encased in ice that was going to prove to be more dangerous than any temper he had seen before. She walked up to him, keeping her eyes on him every step of the way. He warily watched her approach him.

"Just how angry are you, Chloe?" he asked.

She didn't reply with words. Instead, she reared back and punched him in the stomach with her fist as hard as she could. She didn't display the slightest bit of pain as she stepped back. Without saying a word, she walked out of the bungalow. The calm closing of the front door was more disquieting than if she had slammed it.

Dalton was still trying to breathe normally when Nando showed up at the room.

"What happened?" He looked past Dalton at the clothes strewn across the bedroom.

"Hurricane Chloe."

Chapter Fourteen

"Why are you so unhappy if your trip was such a success?" Regina Sumner asked her daughter.

The two had met for lunch a couple days after Chloe returned from Bella Skin's resort with final notes to be typed and the promise of an imminent merger. The fact that her hand had been bandaged was questioned, but she gave no answers. Even now, Regina's gaze flickered over the white bandage.

"It was very stressful," Chloe said with a tight-lipped grimace.

Regina smiled. Thanks to good genes, she didn't look like a woman in her midfifties. Her black hair was only faintly streaked with gray and her heavy work schedule didn't give her time to be lazy. Unlike her mother and daughter, she didn't bother with many beauty aids. Her excuse was a laboratory didn't require a pretty face, only an intelligent mind. Even now, her salt-and-pepper hair was pulled up in a loose knot while her face bore only a trace of lipstick. Her navy sheath wasn't the height of fashion but suited her angular body.

"I talked to Liza, Chloe," she said gently. "I know that Dalton was on the cruise with you."

Her gaze flew up. "I don't want to talk about it."

"About what? The cruise? Your shipwreck or Dalton?"

Chloe toyed with her spinach salad with its hot bacon dressing. At that moment, she would have killed for a piece of chocolate.

"The only person Liza told was me. She said nothing about Dalton to Amanda," Regina went on.

Chloe gave up any pretense of eating her food. She set her fork down. "All I did was make a fool of myself."

"You know, I always liked that boy." Apparently, she had no problem in eating. "The two of you were so much in love, I was positive you hadn't believed in your grandmother's story about a family curse."

"Curse?" She tried to swallow around the lump in her throat. "You mean the one where the Sumner women can't hold on to their men?"

"That's the one. She tried that story with me and I told her it was a Sumner old wives' tale," Regina said.

"But you couldn't . . ." She knew she couldn't finish the statement.

"Darling." Regina smiled at her the way she used to when a young Chloe came to her with stories about finding monsters under her bed. "Your father didn't want to be a dad. I'm sorry, but he decided it would be more fun to live in a commune and raise corn. I wanted to win awards in chemistry. He later moved to Canada to evade the draft and I finished my degree."

"But Amanda couldn't hold on to a man. And you couldn't." Chloe winced as she said the damning words. "And I couldn't hold on to Dalton."

Regina knew her daughter only too well.

"Did Dalton leave that island of his own free will or did you basically throw him off?"

She winced again. "Well . . ."

"You threw him off." Regina shook her head. "Why?"

Chloe looked around as if spies were lurking in every corner of the small restaurant.

"He was going to hit Nando Rossi," she whispered.

Regina leaned across the table and whispered back, "Why?"

"Because Nando thought I'd turned into some sex goddess and wanted to make love to me. I was trying to leave the room before he got out of hand and Dalton was just coming in. The door opened, I fell on the floor and Nando fell on top of me." Chloe saw the scene flash before her eyes again. A glimmer of a smile touched her lips before she recaptured it. "Dalton said he was protecting his wife and I reminded him I hadn't been his spouse for the past six years. Nando overheard us."

"So you decided the best way to save face with Nando was getting Dalton off the island."

Chloe searched her mother's face for comfort but there wasn't any there. Nor was there any condemnation. If she wasn't imagining it, she would swear the expression on Regina's face was pity.

"I didn't sleep with Nando."

"I never thought you did." Regina smiled as she reached across and covered her daughter's hand with hers. "You're an excellent businesswoman, Chloe, but I'm afraid your grandmother and I fell short in teaching you the ins and outs of a good relationship. When you married Dalton, I saw you with a man who perfectly complemented you. I thought for sure the two of you would make it.''

"Until Amanda interfered," she muttered.

Regina heaved a deep sigh. "I was afraid she had something to do with it, but I could never get her to admit to it." She squeezed Chloe's hand. "So why aren't you going after the man?"

Chloe made a face. "After what I did to him, he wouldn't want to see me again."

"You mean after you told him you wanted him to leave the island."

"I mean after I hit him in the stomach and screamed at him," she admitted in a barely audible voice.

Regina stared at Chloe as if she was looking at a stranger. "You screamed at him and you hit him in the stomach," she repeated.

Chloe nodded sheepishly.

"Darling, you never raise your voice," Regina said, awestruck by her daughter's confession. "And you've never struck anyone. In fact, I can't remember you even throwing a temper tantrum as a child."

Chloe's face turned a bright red. "He made me angry. And he lied to me. He deserved that punch in the stomach. I'm sure after all that, he never wants to talk to me again."

"How do you know that?"

She shifted uneasily in her chair. She was rapidly learning confession wasn't necessarily good for the soul.

"I sent the agency a check for his services." She winced at the last word. "It was sent back with a note from Rachel apologizing for her part in the deception."

"Then I suggest you act the part of the hardheaded businesswoman and take the bull by the horns. March on down to where Dalton is living and tell him how much in love with him you are. And you are," she insisted. "A person only has to look at you to know that."

"But the company will always come between us."

"Then look for a little compromise," she advised. "That shouldn't be difficult for you. Have the business and Dalton, too. Six years had to have matured both of you enough to find a way."

"Amanda would have a coronary if she found out Dalton was back in my life."

Regina looked triumphant. "Aha! You do want him back. Then do something about it."

Chloe reared back at her mother's stern order. "Who's the boss here?"

"Who's the mother here?"

Chloe looked down at her salad and knew she wouldn't be able to finish it. But she also knew she would go to Dalton.

"Who's going to tell Amanda?" she asked her mother. "I bet you haven't said one word to her about your own love life."

Now Regina looked uneasy. "I suppose the two of you wouldn't consider eloping again, would you?"

CHLOE PRIDED HERSELF on not backing down from a battle. Even this one.

"You look as if you're going to a funeral," Liza told her, gazing at her black suit with a critical eye.

Chloe had forgone the crisp white blouse she usually wore with the suit and settled for a wisp of lace for the jacket's deep V neckline. She had already looked in her bathroom mirror, smoothed her ruffled curls and reapplied her lipstick. Grateful there wasn't a run in her stocking, she settled herself behind her desk.

"I am. Mine." She moved her calendar a fraction of an inch to the left.

"Don't think of her as your boss. Think of her as your grandmother," Liza told her.

Chloe groaned loudly. "That's right! Make it worse!" She groped inside her desk drawer. At the moment she was ready for chocolate and cigarettes all in one fell swoop.

Liza ran across the room and grabbed her hand. "You can't," she warned. "Not when she's on her way up."

"Good morning!" Amanda swept into the office with the regal demeanor that had intimidated many a man. Her deep purple silk suit could have been a queen's royal robes.

"Mrs. Sumner, you look lovely today," Liza greeted her with a bright smile.

"Thank you, dear." She turned to Chloe who had stood. Amanda brushed her cheek against her granddaughter's. "You really must make an effort to stay out of the sun. Just those few days have effected such damage to your skin." She critically eyed Chloe's exposed neckline as she sat down across from her granddaughter.

"Actually, I might keep the tan. At least, until the end of summer," she said carefully. "I really like the healthier look it gives me."

Amanda's eyes frosted over. "I don't think that would be a good idea. Just because the Europeans seem to prefer bronzed skin doesn't mean we will endorse it." Her gaze immediately warmed. "Speaking of that, I must congratulate you on the contract drawn up with Bella Skin. I knew you and Signor Rossi would get along famously. He was offered a chance to work in our factory and he's accepted."

Chloe froze. "He has?"

The older woman's smile broadened. "With his charm and sales acumen and your business head I see our company growing at an incredible rate."

"You make it sound like another kind of merger." She laughed nervously.

She arched an eyebrow. "Would that be so bad?"

"Yes!" Chloe felt a royal panic attack coming.

"Why? I thought you liked the man. He's certainly attracted to you. I see nothing wrong in the two of you growing close—" she paused delicately "—as long as you're discreet and remember who is in charge."

"But I don't want Nando," she argued.

"Not even if your liaison with him helps the company?" Amanda wasn't pleased with Chloe's protest.

"It isn't good business sense," she suddenly blurted out.

Amanda could have been a statue.

"If nothing else, I do believe my business sense has always been impeccable." She stood, smoothing the wrinkles from her skirt. "Perhaps you better do some hard thinking about this, Chloe."

"We need to talk about this now," Chloe went on.

"I don't think so." Amanda started walking toward the door where Liza hovered in the background. "I also cannot wait until your hair grows out. That short cut isn't you. And it appears your idea of a new wardrobe isn't right, either."

"Grandmother!" Chloe was fast on her heels.

Amanda didn't turn around as she walked through the open doorway. "I suggest we discuss this at a later time when we're both a lot calmer."

"I'm calm now!"

She stopped and turned around to face her granddaughter.

"I'm not."

The moment Amanda was out of sight, Chloe dove for her desk and pulled out the candy box. She stuffed two pieces in her mouth at the same time she drew out a cigarette.

"You are nuts!" Liza walked in.

"I need it." She rummaged through her desk drawer for her cigarette lighter. "Ah! Here it is!" She held it up at the same time Amanda walked back inside.

The older woman took in the guilty expression on the two women's faces, then gazed impassively at the candy box, the cigarette pack and lighter still in Chloe's hand. Liza looked as if she wanted to sink through the floor. Chloe looked as if she wished she were on the other side of the world.

"It appears there are a great many things you haven't told me."

Chloe sensed the time had come and braced herself for Hurricane Amanda.

"Yes, Amanda. I smoke and I eat chocolate," she announced, deciding to get that part over with. Once that confession was out of the way, telling her about Dalton should be a breeze. "I've kept it a secret from you too long. Don't worry, I won't do either in public."

"I should hope not. We at Chrysalis have always spoken out about good health equaling good skin."

"There's more." She decided it was time to plunge in.

Her eyes narrowed. "Such as?"

"Dalton and I have reconciled. He was on the cruise with me," she blurted out.

Amanda's face could have been carved from stone as she faced her granddaughter. Until the faintest of movements crossed her nose as if she smelled something bad.

"You are back with that artist?" She said it as if that was equally bad.

"Yes, I am and I didn't appreciate hearing you kept him away from me when we were separated."

"It was for your own good."

Chloe shook her head, not all that amazed her grandmother saw it that way. "That's the problem, Amanda, you always did what *you* thought was for my own good. You never let me find out for myself. You may as well know now there's going to be some changes made. First with Dalton and me getting back together." *At least they would as soon as she went to him and apologized.* "I'll be keeping the short hair and my new clothes because I like them. Chrysalis will also be moving forward." She picked up a bound sheaf of papers off the top of her desk and handed it to Amanda. "This is an outline for new products and looks. I'll be presenting them to the board next week."

Amanda thumbed through the pages, occasionally stopping to read.

"We'll let the board decide on this," she said finally.

"Without your negative attitude," she warned. "Let them do this for themselves."

Amanda looked up at Chloe, seeing herself more than forty years ago.

"You really intend to remarry that man?"

"That man's name is Dalton and, yes, I do. And this time there will be no interfering from you."

"I wonder if putting you under a doctor's care would help," Amanda mused.

Chloe threw up her hands. "We're discussing my life, Amanda. Smoking, chocolate and all. Now maybe I'll give up smoking, but I *will not* give up my chocolate! And I won't give up Dalton. We need to be together and, this time, you won't separate us. Besides," she added slyly, "there could be a great-granddaughter for you to mold in your image."

Amanda looked at her with a considering frown. "Are you pregnant?"

"Not yet."

"Are we talking a bargaining point?"

Chloe had to smile. "No, we're talking about you and Dalton acting like relatives instead of enemies. Do you think you can handle that?"

Amanda's shoulders rose and fell in a deep sigh. "If he dares call me Mandy I will walk out of the room."

Her smile grew broader. "I don't think he will."

"And he will wear a tie when he comes to my home."

"I don't think he will."

Amanda always believed in backpedaling when there was a chance she was losing the battle. That way she could regroup her inner forces for later.

"He is good-looking in a raw, male way. Perhaps he'll consider acting as a model for our men's line."

"I don't think so, but I'll mention it to him." Chloe threw her arms around her grandmother. "Don't worry, everything will be fine."

"That's easy for you to say."

"Now would you like to hear about my deciding to keep my travel to a minimum and working late will be done at home?"

Amanda heaved a sigh. She walked back to Chloe's desk and sat down in the visitor's chair. "Let's talk."

"SEVENTEEN D. Seventeen D," Chloe muttered to herself, comparing the number written on the piece of paper in her hand to the ones on the buildings along the sidewalk. The ornate metal numbers written in an elegant old-fashioned scroll were difficult to read under the streetlights. Once she found the street number she was looking for, she had to hunt for a parking spot next. She held her breath as her bumper got a little too close to a Ford Explorer as she eased her car against the sidewalk.

Chloe hadn't called first to see if Dalton was home. Seeing lights burning on the fourth floor assured her she didn't have to worry as she walked up the steps.

Again, she was in luck when someone walked out as she approached the door and she quickly grabbed it so she wouldn't have to buzz Dalton.

Now all she had to do was hope he would let her past his front door. And she prayed he would listen to her.

What she didn't expect was the prospect of walking three steep flights of stairs in high heels. By the second flight she was limping and cursing her shoes.

"I was a fool to do all this," she muttered, pulling on her short skirt and bending down to slip off her shoes.

By the time she reached the door marked D, she was breathing hard and holding her side. She pressed the doorbell and leaned against the wall while she tried to catch her breath. She had just remembered to slip her shoes back on when the door flew open.

"Dammit, I can't be coming to the door every—" Dalton's voice dropped off when he saw his visitor. He wiped all expression from his face.

"Can I come in?"

She had no idea it was the uncertainty on her face that stopped him from closing the door in her face.

"Why not?" He stepped back and swept his arm out in a grand gesture. "Please, come in."

She ignored his mocking tone and limped inside.

Dalton looked down at her shoes and cocked an eyebrow. "You didn't walk up in those, did you?"

"Suffered more likely," she muttered, looking around with interest.

Being the top floor, the ceiling was three-quarters glass. Chloe noticed the apartment was actually two levels, with what appeared to be Dalton's studio above them. Rice-paper screens divided the living room from the kitchen and she could catch a glimpse of an un-made bed over in one corner.

"This is very nice." She eyed the large plump sofa, an off-white nubby fabric affair with rust, hunter green and dark brown throw pillows tossed against the back.

"Why are you here, Chloe?" Dalton asked tiredly.

She spun around and noticed the weariness in his features. The tired lines in his body. She noticed his jeans had dabs of dark clay on them and his T-shirt looked as if it belonged in the trash. His dark hair hung loose and she doubted he had shaved in the past couple days. She wasn't surprised to see him barefoot.

"I treated you badly at the resort," she began, rubbing her hands together nervously which only brought his gaze down to them.

"What happened to your hand?"

Chloe blushed and quickly hid the bandaged hand behind her back. "A bad sprain," she muttered.

A hint of a smile touched his lips as he thought of the bruise coloring his stomach because she had punched him so hard. For once, he didn't feel any sympathy for her. "Really?"

She glared at him, irritated he was finding it so amusing. "Really."

"Good because you left a pretty good bruise. Want to see?" He started to lift the hem of his shirt.

"No!" She stepped forward with a hand outstretched to stop him. She stepped back when he stopped. "Dalton, I'm sorry I blew up at you at the resort. After the days we'd spent alone it was natural we'd start to fall back into thinking we were husband and wife."

"It looks as if I was the only one who thought that."

Chloe removed her shoes and dropped them on the floor. "No, I started thinking that way too," she said in a low voice. "But when we arrived at the resort, I knew I had the merger to worry about and I made the mistake I vowed not to make. I put us on the back burner. Nando started the Italian lover routine and I thought I could handle it. Then I got mad when you took care of it for me."

His features darkened. "I wanted to deck him."

She winced. "I know. And Nando knew it. He finally admitted he was wrong in making a pass at me, but he felt he had to do it to keep his reputation."

"Yeah, he told me that already," he muttered. "He called me to say he understood why and apologized for making a pass at you. Tell Liza to be careful because he thinks she's pretty hot stuff. But that isn't telling me why you're here."

Chloe took a deep breath in hopes it would shore up her courage. "I came here to apologize for my behavior and I hope we can try again. This time with better results."

"What makes you think I'm willing to try again? I've been kicked in the teeth twice by you, Chloe. I'm not a masochist who wants to see it happen again." He threw up his hands. He still looked tired and a bit out of sorts. "I'm sorry. I love you, but right now it's not easy imagining living with you if you're going to revert to Ms. Corporate America every time there's a deal on the table. I was willing to share you with your work, but you have to do some sharing, too. And I'm talking about sharing yourself."

She looked around as she tried to formulate her thoughts. She hadn't expected this to be easy. But she hadn't wanted him to give her a hard time, either. A form in a corner of the room caught her eye and she walked over to it.

"Oh, Dalton." The words were soft with awe as she studied the delicate figurine of a woman. She had no idea what medium had been used until she studied it further and realized it was crafted from a creamy-colored marble. There was no denying the face was hers. And no denying the figure had been molded with a great deal of love.

Tears blurred her vision when she carefully touched the figurine's flowing hair and traced the lines of the sliplike gown covering the body.

"That was the first piece I made after we divorced," he said quietly, coming up to stand behind her.

She stared at the figurine because it was easier than looking at Dalton. "I stood up to Amanda."

He stilled. "And?"

She smiled at the memory. "She hates the short hair, the change in my wardrobe and she especially dislikes my eating chocolate and smoking. She talked about putting me under a doctor's care to 'kick the habit.'" She smiled wryly.

"And?" Wariness colored his voice.

Chloe took a deep breath and turned around. She looked up to meet his gaze.

"And I told Amanda it's my life and I'll eat chocolate if I want to. And if you'll have me again, I'd like to rearrange my priorities and share the rest of my life with you," she said.

He didn't move to give away his thoughts.

"And?"

"Will you stop saying that word! All right." She moved around him and began pacing the floor. She desperately wanted chocolate and a cigarette, not necessarily in that order. "I will leave your toothpaste tube alone."

This time he didn't say a word. He just stood there with his arms crossed in front of his chest, looking as much like a statue as the figurine next to him.

"And I'll work at keeping traveling to a minimum, and if I have to work late I'll bring it home with me." She shot him a quick glance, but he wasn't allowing her to see his thoughts. "And I'll learn to cook. But you have to make some allowances here, too!"

"I'll keep my channel surfing down to a minimum and I'll shower before going to bed," he told her. "Dirty socks will end up in the hamper and damp towels hung up."

Chloe was greedy. She wanted to hear more.

"And?" she asked.

He waited a beat before continuing. "And this time you won't be allowed to run back to Grandma when things get rough. We'll battle it out to the finish. But there will be no end for us." He fixed her with a steely look. "If we're getting married again, Chloe Sumner, you will take my name and it will be forever."

Laughter bubbled up her throat. "And?"

Dalton walked toward her with surefooted grace. "And I'd like us to have a couple kids," he said huskily.

Her laughter died. "Oh, Dalton," she whispered, throwing her arms around him. "Yes."

"Dame Amanda won't have any say in raising them except as a grandmother," he warned her.

"She already thinks I'm crazy. I don't think anything else will surprise her now."

He took away any other words she was going to say by kissing her deeply. By the time he finished, she was clinging weakly to him.

"We will make this work," Dalton said fiercely.

Chloe looked up at him with love shining from her eyes. "I guess I didn't need to wear the sexy dress."

He looked down at the off-the-shoulder red knit dress that clung to her curves. "I'm not complaining." He held on to her shoulders and began backing his way toward the bedroom. "Besides, I want to see how easy it will be to get you out of it and into my bed."

"We'll fight," she warned, not unwilling to go with him.

"And we'll make up."

"And what if that doesn't work?" Chloe felt the need to play devil's advocate. "What if we come to a point where neither one of us wants to give in? I agree with you. I don't want us to split up again, either."

Dalton's smile warmed her all the way down to her toes. "Then I guess we'll just have to find ourselves another island."

Turn the page for a bonus look at what's in store for you in the next 1-800-HUSBAND book.

It's a sneak preview of

HER TWO HUSBANDS
by Mollie Molay
September 1995

"Whether you want him for business... or pleasure, for one month or one night, we have the husband you've been looking for. When circumstances dictate the appearance of a man in your life, call 1-800-HUSBAND for an uncomplicated, uncompromising solution. Call now. Operators standing by..."

Don't miss #597 HER TWO HUSBANDS by Mollie Molay!

Chapter One

"Do you have a husband, Katie?"

"No." Katie felt her face redden, as she regarded Neil Gibson, the chief executive director of Toyland Industries, whose chin was braced on two well-manicured forefingers. "Why do you ask?"

He held up the pastel pink brochure for The Tickle Pink Inn in Carmel. "I take it you're proposing we hold our conference in a honeymoon hotel? A bit unusual, wouldn't you say?"

"That's the point, sir." Katie straightened with pride. "I know this meeting must remain secret. No one would think to look for a business conference in this type of location."

Gibson paused to consider the point. "You're absolutely right about that. However..." He glanced back down at the brochure. "If you were to go by yourself, it might arouse suspicions. We can't have that, can we?"

"We can't?" was all Katie could manage. The hairs on the back of her neck tingled when she connected his earlier question about her romantic status with the calculated look that came across his face. She sensed something awful was about to happen when he pressed his intercom.

A deep voice answered. "Smith here."

"Come in my office for a minute, Dak. I have someone I want you to meet."

Katie's sixth sense went into overdrive. At the knock on the door, she braced herself for trouble.

The door opened and Dakota Smith entered. She'd seen the man many times around the building, and from the first time she'd laid eyes on him he'd captured her interest and she'd sensed his animal magnetism. His self-assurance enveloped him like a cloak as he swept past her and sat down. The burgundy leather upholstery formed a perfect backdrop for his sun-drenched brown hair and tanned features. She couldn't help but stare.

"Dak, I'd like you to meet Katie O'Connor. She's got some great ideas for this year's conference."

His eyes bore into hers. "Perhaps you didn't know that was my job?"

Gibson interjected. "Let me tell you about it." He handed Dak the brochure and explained all about Katie's outlandish plan.

"Have it your way, then," Dak said when he was done. "Just make certain everyone appears to be on some kind of honeymoon."

"Glad you feel that way." Gibson nodded complacently. "Because I brought you in to tell you that I expect you to attend the conference along with Katie."

Dak's gaze swung from his boss to Katie. She felt a ripple of apprehension when a faint smile curved at his lips and he eyed her with interest. "Sure. No problem."

Who did this man think he was? Katie silently fumed. He might think he was God's gift to women, but he certainly wasn't hers.

"There is one hitch." Gibson leaned back in his chair. "Given the circumstances, you'll have to go as husband and wife."

"Count me out!" Dak snorted and surged out of his chair.

Katie gathered her materials and prepared to leave. "I wouldn't go as this man's wife if you paid me to do it!"

"That's just the point, Ms. O'Connor." Gibson's voice was well modulated. "I *am* paying you. Now, if you'll both just calm down. I'm not suggesting anything more than the appearance of a marriage. Be seen together, hold hands, share a room..."

Katie glanced over at Dak, whose frustration was visible in his clenched fists and in the way his hazel eyes bored into hers. Not even for the sake of her job could she see herself sharing a room—a bed?—with this man. But what could she do?

"The truth is, Mr. Gibson, I—I'm... already married." Where did that come from? "Yes! Uh, you see, we've kept it secret... for personal reasons. But I see now that it's best to let you know, under the circumstances."

"Don't see why you've kept it secret, O'Connor, but have it your way. In any case, it's no problem." At Gibson's approval, Katie finally let out the breath she'd been holding. "Just bring him along."

Oh, what a tangled web we weave...

Katie felt as if she'd been punched in the stomach. She'd just gone from bad to worse. She looked over to Dak's face, and from the look in his piercing eyes, she knew she had only one choice: She had to find a husband . . . and fast.

But where?

* * * * *

*Don't miss the next installment in
the* 1-800-HUSBAND *miniseries!
Watch for American Romance #597*
HER TWO HUSBANDS *by Mollie Molay—
available in September 1995.*

HARLEQUIN®

AMERICAN ◆ ROMANCE®

Once in a while, there's a story so special, a story so unusual,
that your pulse races, your blood rushes. We call this

AMERICAN
ROMANCE
heart
beat

HART'S DREAM is one such story.

At first they were dreams—strangely erotic. Then visions—strikingly real. Ever since his accident, when Dr. Sara Carr's sweet voice was his only lifeline, Daniel Hart couldn't get the woman off his mind. Months later it was more than a figment of his imagination calling to him, luring him, doing things to him that only a flesh-and-blood woman could…. But Sara was nowhere to be found….

#589 HART'S DREAM
by
Mary Anne Wilson

Available in July wherever Harlequin books are sold. Watch for more Heartbeat stories, coming your way—only from American Romance!

IT'S A BABY BOOM!

NEW ARRIVALS

We're expecting—again! Join us for a reprisal of the New Arrivals promotion, in which special American Romance authors invite you to read about equally special heroines—all of whom are on a nine-month adventure! We expect each mom-to-be will find the man of her dreams—and a daddy in the bargain!

Watch for the newest arrival!

#600 ANGEL'S BABY
by Pamela Browning
September 1995

PRIZE SURPRISE SWEEPSTAKES!

This month's prize:

BEAUTIFUL WEDGWOOD CHINA!

This month, as a special surprise, we're giving away a bone china dinner service for eight by Wedgwood**, one of England's most prestigious manufacturers!

Think how beautiful your table will look, set with lovely Wedgwood china in the casual Countryware pattern! Each five-piece place setting includes dinner plate, salad plate, soup bowl and cup and saucer.

The facing page contains two Entry Coupons (as does every book you received this shipment). Complete and return *all* the entry coupons; **the more times you enter, the better your chances of winning!**

Then keep your fingers crossed, because you'll find out by September 15, 1995 if you're the winner!

Remember: The more times you enter, the better your chances of winning!*